REPOSSESSION is the third in a series of stories about Joe Anderson, a former naval officer who is lovingly devoted to Mary Johnston, but cannot resist the allure of the sea or the challenge of dangerous covert quests for the CIA. In this adventure the impossible turns on humorous events as Mary and her outlandish friend Frances get in the way.

OTHER NOVELS BY STEVE COLEMAN

The Navigator:
A Perilous Passage, Evasion at Sea

The Navigator II:
Irish Revenge

André's Reboot:
Striving to Save Humanity

THE
• NAVIGATOR •
III

REPOSSESSION

STEVE COLEMAN

BIRMINGHAM, ALABAMA

Cover, Interior, eBook Design by The Book Cover Whisperer: OpenBookDesign.biz

Stephen B. Coleman, Publisher
Birmingham, AL
steve@captstevestories.com

www.Stephenbcoleman.com
www.captstevestories.com

Library of Congress Control Number: 2021922857

978-0-9850065-3-2 Paperback
978-0-9850065-7-0 eBook

Printed in the United States of America

FIRST EDITION

• ACKNOWLEDGEMENTS •

I WOULD LIKE TO THANK especially Cesci Llorente Fowler for her grand assistance editing the lines of Spanish dialogue. I also wish to thank the members of Carolynne Scott's Fiction Critique. Authors Carolynne Scott, Jackie Walburn, Ron Carter, Willum Fowler, Chervis Isom, and David Roberts provided outstanding criticism, suggestions, and encouragement. My fabulous friends, Tom and Gail Cosby, and Roger Carlisle, along with the fine poets of Highland Avenue Eaters of Words were great supporters. Eladio Ruiz de Molina and Dan Belser gave me valuable information about Cuba. Retired naval officers Doyle Hodges and Harb Moore graciously assisted with Joe's flashback aboard a frigate. My dearest sister, Wodie Monaghan, and my wonderful wife, Sumter, offered much loving encouragement and support. Christine Horner designed a most artistic and attractive book cover and interior layout. Many thanks and love to all.

Steve Coleman
November 8, 2021

• PRELUDE •

A t the commercial piers of Havana, Cuba on a sweat-soaking sunny, humid mid-day of July 15th, 2019, the aluminum handrails of the ship's gangway were nearly too hot to touch. Ten handcuffed American crewmen stumbled down the steps, insulted by the shouts and jabs of rifle butts by soldiers of the *Fuerzas Armadas Revolucionarias*. Last in line, the captain of the merchant ship, *Sea Urchin*, protested vigorously. He was forced onto the gangway but hesitated to walk down. A soldier hit him with a rifle butt in the small of his back, sending him tumbling to the pier. Other troops grabbed the wounded and bleeding captain, dragged him to their truck and threw him in with the rest of the crew. As the vehicle drove away, two remaining soldiers began setting up a guard post at the base of the gangway of the seized and impounded ship.

• CHAPTER ONE •

Lightning lit the heavy gray afternoon clouds of July 24, 2019. Booming thunder rattled the window-ports, and heavy raindrops drummed on the weather decks of boats moored in the boat yard at Stuart, Florida. Joe Anderson's sport fishing boat strained on its lines, its PVC fenders periodically bumping the wooden pier. Joe lay on his back, his head and shoulders under the galley sink, struggling to remove a corroded rusting drainpipe. Running through his mind was the earlier phone conversation with Mary Johnston, the lovely widow who adored him.

"I think about you all the time, Joe. When are you coming home?"

It was calling her house "home" that gave him pause. It was the home she had shared with her wealthy late husband. Widowed for three years and having become attached to Joe now, she expected Joe to come fill Earnest's place. Joe's great affection for Mary blossomed during a treacherous sea adventure together. His attraction to her was not much related either to her residence or her wealthy southern life of leisure in Birmingham. Some years ago, Joe had experienced a similar homelife in a first marriage, which soon became a painful failure.

"Got to finish a few more repairs," Joe replied, avoiding her meaning. Neither spoke for a few moments.

"Why do you waste your time repairing that boat," she said. "You could be here playing tennis, or golf, swimming in the pool. There are a couple of outdoor barbecues with friends coming up. Wouldn't that be fun?"

"I know it's hard to understand, but *Tartan* is more than just a boat to me." He glanced at his framed photo of Hemingway on the dock at Key West showing off an eight-foot marlin. It hung prominently on the bulkhead behind the settee next to a youthful portrait of himself in his naval officer's blue uniform.

"I wish you would come down, meet me in Fort Lauderdale. We can make a fun run to Nassau or Eleuthera maybe. I'm working hard on repairing everything…"

"Isn't it hurricane season?" she asked.

"A little early yet. We should be okay."

"I don't completely share your optimism," she said and paused. "But we seem to spend too much time apart, Joe. I just want to be with you."

"I sure miss you. I hope you'll break away from everything and come enjoy a cruise." Joe crossed his fingers and waited.

"When do you want me to come?" she asked finally.

"Come this weekend. There's a direct flight for you to take on Friday at 6:20." He waited for her reply.

"Then afterwards, you'll come to Birmingham for a nice long stay?" There was a long pause before he replied.

"If that's what will make you happy."

"Promise?"

Joe threw his hands up in consternation, then sighed, glad she couldn't see his gesture. "I promise."

When they ended the call, he wondered how two people could be so much in love and yet prefer such different lifestyles. Letting out a deep breath, he went back to work.

Deciding after several futile attempts to loosen the fitting, threatening to use his cutting torch to open the joint, he pulled himself out. A car horn sounded on the pier. Standing and peering through the streams of rain running down the forward porthole, he saw a yellow cab outside and a short, balding middle-aged man climbing out. It was Stan Adams, his old handler from CIA, whom he hadn't heard from in months.

"Adams? My god, what does he want?"

Shaking his head with irritation, Joe wiped his hands and brushed back his untrimmed hair. Adams' unexpected arrival was untimely to say the least. Hoping to complete repairs quickly he wanted move to the luxurious Hurricane Hole Marina in Fort Lauderdale, wanting Mary's first view of his boat to be in the best of surroundings. This was no time for interruptions.

He watched Adams hurrying onto the dock carrying a briefcase in one hand and an umbrella in the other. A gust of wind caught the underside of the black umbrella, turning it wrong side out. He threw the thing in the water with disgust and hurried on. With a chuckle Joe went up to greet him.

"How'd you find me?" he demanded as Adams climbed aboard.

The agent tapped Joe's breast pocket where his iPhone was. "We are CIA, you know."

"I ought to keep the damn thing turned off."

Adams grinned. "You might miss out on something." He glanced upward and squinted. "Say, can we get out of the rain?"

Joe grimaced, took the man's briefcase and led him into the forward cabin. Adams grabbed his damp flower-print shirt, pulled it away from his chest and shook it.

"Glad you dressed for the occasion," Joe quipped. "Want a towel?" The CIA handler nodded, plopped down behind the table and looked around.

"Nice boat."

"It's home." Joe went to the head for a towel, tossed it to Adams, moved some dirty dishes off the table, and sat across from his visitor.

"So, why am I graced by your unannounced and, may I say, somewhat untimely arrival?"

The handler smiled like a used car salesman. "We want you to make a little sea cruise."

Joe shook his head. "First off, I'm not ready for another of your assignments. I may never be ready." He grabbed the neckline of his tee-shirt and pulled it over, exposing the gunshot scar on his shoulder. "I still have this little I.R.A. memento from Northern Ireland." He could not suppress the memory of Fiona's brother Tim shooting him as he escaped.

"Well, I have a scar, too, from about fifteen years ago," Adams said, "but let's not get into a who's-is-bigger discussion." He put his briefcase on the table. "You can still navigate a big boat can't you?" Adams asked.

"What kind of boat?"

"It's a cargo kind of thing—about two hundred feet long or so…"

"That's a small ship, not a boat."

"Okay, a ship then. But it's pretty-well automated I'm told, so that you don't have to have a lot of crew."

"Until there's trouble, and then you better have lots of crew. What is this, and why me? I mean, there's lots of mariners around looking for captains' jobs."

"It takes someone with your kind of security clearance because of what's aboard."

"A spy ship or something, huh? Wait, stop! Don't tell me. There's "need to know" and then there's "don't fucking want to know.""

"Look man, here's the deal. You probably read about some U.S. diplomats in Cuba having their hearing damaged. The embassy got hit with a strange low frequency sound. We assumed it came from some new kind of weapon used by the Cubans or their Russian cohorts.

So the President ordered a covert investigation. NSA installed electronics surveillance equipment, and we had a CIA crew take the ship to Havana."

"Cuba allowed that?"

"*El presidente* invited us to investigate this acoustic... weapon, or whatever, but then he put restrictions on what our people could see and do. So we sent in this seemingly innocuous merchant ship secretly equipped with electronic listening gear. As a ruse, the captain bought a load of rum, which would be delivered from a local distillery. While waiting on the shipment, they were able to carry out their surveillance mission—with negative results, by the way. It's still a mystery."

"Then why didn't the crew just sail away in this Trojan Horse of yours?

Adams grinned cynically. "The rum was bought and loaded on the ship," he said. "But there was one problem. Our captain got his back up and refused to make an under-the-table payment. The port authority retaliated by seizing and impounding the boat...ship. They arrested and deported our crew."

"Sounds like a reasonable thing for them to do," Joe laughed. "Hell, that's what I would've done. So why doesn't our State Department just negotiate a deal?"

"After all those new blustery declarations and embargos against Cuba?" Adams grimaced.

"I thought we were enjoying better relations recently. What happened?"

"Cuba is supporting Maduro in Venezuela, destabilizing the Americas, and who knows what all," Adams said. "We—the CIA—told State that Cuba lacked the military and economic resources to threaten anybody, much less the U. S." He shook his head. "But our brilliant Administration won't listen. Who knows what these politicians have to gain."

"Pretty straight talk from a career man, Adams," Joe replied. "You 'Virginia Farm boys' must be a bit unhappy with our president."

"That's another story." He shook his head. "Anyway, let's get back to your mission."

"Don't call it my mission." He got up and walked into the galley. "As I said, let the State Department negotiate over this ship of yours. Maybe the president can tweet it out of there or something. What's your hurry anyway?"

"Because all that takes time we haven't got," Adams replied. "The electronic gear is hidden behind some false bulkheads. If the Cubans start poking around and find the spy stuff, it not only compromises our equipment, it'd be a political disaster."

"Just another snafu in international relations," Joe quipped. "You have got a problem." He opened a cabinet near the fridge. "Will you have coffee or anything?"

"Got any scotch? It's already been a long day."

"Sure."

The older man watched in silence as Joe found two almost clean but filmy plastic glasses and a fifth of Usher's.

"How many employees has CIA got now? 50,000? I'd think you'd have a few hundred regulars to draw from for this project."

"No one else is a former surface warfare naval officer, boat captain, and CIA operative. You're kind of a unique son of a bitch."

"All that's past now," Joe replied. He brought the scotch, sat down and poured a healthy shot in each glass.

Adams glanced at the engine parts lying on a drop cloth, the wrenches and open toolbox near the sink, and the pile of dirty clothes that were lending body odor to the surroundings. He picked up his glass and pointed to the portrait photo of "Lieutenant Commander Anderson."

"You won a medal or two in Desert Storm, didn't you?" Adams asked.

"I was just proficient," Joe replied. His thoughts flashed back to the night in January 1991 when he was Tactical Action Officer in the combat information center of a guided missile frigate on patrol ten miles from Kuwait Bay in the Persian Gulf. He idly was observing the Situation Plot when something new appeared.

New contact designated Skunk Alpha, bearing three-zero-two," the *surface search radar operator called out, "range sixteen thousand six hundred yards. Constant bearing, decreasing range." Joe digested the information for five heartbeats. Not having detected the contact until it was eight miles away meant it must be small. Intelligence reports indicated Iraq had missile-armed patrol boats in the area.*

"*Weps, acquire Alpha.," Joe ordered. A twenty second silence seemed forever.*

"*Locked on and tracking with the Mark 92," the Weapons Officer replied. "Phalanx in acquisition mode."*

Joe keyed the 21MC intercom to the Officer of the Deck. "Bridge, Combat: Recommend coming to course zero-niner-zero, all engines ahead flank, ASAP. See if you can get eyeballs on Skunk Alpha at three-zero-two, eight miles" He walked over to the red captain's phone and pressed the buzzer. Then the electronic warfare operator on the SLQ-12 spoke.

"*Detecting a fire control radar painting us from bearing two-niner-five."*

The fire control radar emission was enough indication the enemy already could have fired a missile flying low over the water and all but undetectable.

"*Weps: Fire chaff. Verify the Phalanx is engaging." As he gave his order, there was an almost immediate 'FOOMP, FOOMP' from the SRBOC chaff cannons. The captain charged into CIC, and Joe turned to speak to him, but the old man was giving a thumbs up.*

"*Batteries released. Kill the fucker." The captain's voice was interrupted by the rumbling, vibrating buzz of the Phalanx firing a hundred rounds, soon followed by a shock wave from the port quarter as the enemy Exocet missile exploded.*

"Target Alpha bears two-eight-six, range fourteen thousand, eight hundred," said the surface search operator.

"Mark 75 locked on Alpha, ready to fire," Weapons Officer reported. Joe glanced at his captain, who only nodded.

"Aft Gun released," Joe ordered. "Kill target Alpha."

A staccato sound of 76mm rounds spat from the Mark 75 after gun mount. The projectiles arced slightly across the Gulf, requiring approximately 17 seconds to arrive at their target, obliterating the Iraqi patrol craft.

"Combat, Bridge," the OOD called. "Lookouts report a white-hot explosion, believed to be target Alpha."

A cheer rose from the CIC crew. Joe glanced at the captain, who wore a look of mock disgust.

"Anderson, is that all you woke me up for?" Then he winked and shook Joe's hand.

• • •

"WHAT ARE YOU GRINNING about?" Adams asked. I thought you were a million miles away.

Joe shook his head, a faint smile still on his lips. "Just remembering," he said. The present came back in focus, and he glanced around at *Tartan's* junked-up salon. Adams noted and seemed to guess his thoughts.

"To younger days," Adams said. "Younger days and better times." Joe nodded and took a another swig of whiskey.

Adams picked up his own drink and took a sip. He opened his briefcase, extracted an 8x10 photo and passed it over. Joe studied the satellite photo and took a swallow of scotch.

"Typical looking tramp steamer, I'd say," he decided. "2,500 tons give or take. What's that name on the bow?

"*Sea Urchin.*"

"Oh, that's a nice name for a spy ship."

Adams ignored the sarcasm. "As you can see, it's docked at a pier in Havana, not heavily guarded."

"Listen, Stan, what makes you think anybody could take it away from them?"

"Let me show you something," Adams said. He extracted a newspaper page from the briefcase. "Here's an article in *The New York Times* from a few months ago. It describes several ship captains who make a living by going to third-world ports and using force or subterfuge to bring back vessels that have been seized or pirated or whatever. We figure you're good enough to bring our ship back the same way."

"Oh, thanks for the compliment," Joe said with a smirk. "Just go repossess it, huh? The way these wrecker guys go slip in at night and pick up cars out of driveways with the owner shooting as they drive away? No thank you."

"Come on, hot shot, you're slicker than that. All you have to do is take it outside the twelve-mile limit and then it's yours."

"And the Cubans will just wave bye-bye as I go? You must be crazy!" Joe laughed. "Or you think I am. Look, Adams, ole buddy, if you came down here just for this, you've got your head up where it's dark and spooky. Here I am, about to enjoy a few days with the dearest woman I've ever met. You don't know how hard I've been working to get her here. If I renege on our weekend plans, she'll have a fit." He shook his head emphatically. "There's no way I'm going on some wild mission like this."

Adams emptied his glass and poured them both another shot.

"If we don't get that ship out of there before the commies start sniffing around and find our gear, we're up the creek. It was CIA's blunder, and CIA has to get it out of there."

Adams reached across and grabbed Joe's wrist. "You have every qualification."

"And no brains, apparently." Joe pulled his arm away. "You think I can just slip aboard, get that thing underway, and steam out of the harbor? And what are the Cubans going to be doing? Singing 'Anchors Away' *en Español* and waving, *Adios, amigos*? And besides, I don't know anything about whatever engine it has. It takes a trained man to run it."

"We've got a topnotch German engineer from Caterpillar to go with you."

"Topnotch, huh? Look, Adams, this is nuts. You people are out of your minds."

Adams reached in the briefcase again and pulled out a satellite photo of Havana harbor and laid it on the table.

"As you can see, it's docked fairly close to the harbor entrance," the handler said. "Not a long run out to sea."

"Bull shit," Joe said. " and put his finger on the chart. "See that naval base here and that old castle up on the cliff? Morro Castle, I think it's called. What kind of guns do you think are up there guarding the harbor entrance?" He stood up and fiddled with putting tools away.

"This is an urgent matter of national security," Adams went on, following him with his eyes. "We've considered all other possibilities. This is the best damn shot we have." He reached in the briefcase again, pulled out a plane ticket and reached it toward Joe. "Let's get on down to Key West where we can plan this thing out."

Joe stared at the ticket as if it were a rattlesnake. "When?" he asked.

"Right now," the other replied. "These are for the 3:50 flight to Key West."

"You ARE crazy," Joe said. "Just drop everything and go like I have nothing going on here." He mimed holding a phone to his ear. "Hello, Mary. Guess what, you can't come visit because I have to go to

Cuba and steal a ship." He threw his hand down and stared at Adams. "Jeez, you must think I'm the one who's crazy."

"It'll just be for a day or so," the handler said. He gave Joe a calculating look and gritted his teeth. "Shit, we'll pay three hundred thousand, and don't try to negotiate. That's my absolute limit." He picked up the bottle and filled Joe's glass. "Look at yourself, pal. Working like a trojan, grease on your pants, likely going into debt trying to restore this boat. Is this the real you, Joe? I don't think so."

Joe eased back down in his seat, took up his glass and gulped.

"What you need is to get out on the water, involved in a good adventure," Adams went on. "That's who you are, and it's where you ought to be. Hell, you even speak a little Spanish." He leaned toward Joe. "All you have to do is go see the whole plan. You can refuse if you don't like it. But, if you do it, I'll get you that three hundred thou and be on the pier with the check when you dock the ship in Miami." He reached across the table and gave Joe's arm a light punch. "Aw, come on, ANDERSON. This mission has your name all over it."

• • •

JOE PHONED THE MARINA office to say his boat would remain docked for a week or so. As he dressed and packed a small bag, he helped Adams finish off most of the bottle of scotch. They were in the taxi and almost to the airport before Joe summoned the courage to call Mary.

"Hey, Joe honey!" she answered cheerily. "I'm over at Frances Smith's house playing bridge."

"That's nice."

"I've already bought my ticket to Lauderdale, arriving Friday afternoon at 4:00. Can you meet me there? Then we can go to that great seafood restaurant you took me to in April. Gosh, I'm getting excited! Aren't you, Joe?" There was a pause of excruciating length.

"Mary," he said finally, "I have something... to say... to tell you."

"Have you been drinking?"

"No. I mean, well just one or two. But look, I'm afraid something's come up. It's uh… somebody came down today."

"Who?"

"Stan Adams," Joe said. "He uh…"

"You mean, that man from CIA?" she interrupted. "I thought you couldn't stand him. What does he want?"

"He needs my help with something. He just wants me to go off for a little while."

"Go off? You mean go somewhere? When?"

"Well, right now, sort of." He took a deep breath. "Plane leaves here at 3:50."

"What? Today? Now?" Her voice was becoming animated. "You'll still be back to pick me up on Friday afternoon?"

"I'm so sorry. I've agreed to… well… I'll be paid a lot!"

"To do what, Joe? This better not be some kind of mission or something."

"Oh, they just want me to do a project for them. Nothing very…"

"Watch what you say," Adams whispered in his ear and nodded toward the driver. Joe waved him away.

"Are you telling me you can't meet me on Friday?"

"Mary, I…"

"Oh, Joe, how on earth could you?"

"Now, Mary, babe" he pled. "It's just very important, and necessary."

"And I'm not, is that it? When are you going to be back? Or maybe you're never coming back. I don't know…"

"It's not so bad, really it's not. I'll be all right. I'm just going to… "

"Shhh!" Adams warned. "Don't say where."

"I cannot believe this!"

"It's all right, Mary," Joe said. "I have to do this." There was only silence. He lowered the phone from his ear. "She's hung up on me." He started to call back, but what more could he say?

• CHAPTER TWO •

Afrer clicking off her phone, Mary convulsed into tears. Standing in the hallway at Frances Smith's beautiful home beside the country club golf course, she collected herself, wiped her eyes and tried to contain her anger. In a few moments, she shook her head in irritation and tried to walk casually back to the living room where Frances sat at the card table dealing a new hand of Double Dummy two-handed bridge.

"Did I hear you talking to Joe?" she asked pleasantly.

"Yes," Mary said as evenly as she could. She resumed her seat across the table, picked up her gin and tonic, swizzled the mint sprig around and took a big swallow.

"When are you and Joe going to get married?" Frances asked, picking up her hand and not looking up. "This living in sin is doing nothing for your social standing, Mary dear. I know you don't like my saying it, but I can assure you it's so. One spade."

"Cultural norms have changed," Mary defended. Her friend was likely to say without true malice nearly anything. She looked down at her cards with distraction. "Two diamonds." Her voice waivered.

Frances glanced at Mary's tearstained cheeks with surprise. "Mary? I'll be. Did that Joe Anderson upset you? Why, I'll bet he did!"

Mary laid her cards down. "He said he's going on some kind of mission. Another one! Again! They are so dangerous! I'm so mad I could scream."

"Men are such unfeeling, impetuous fools. Four hearts."

"And not only that, my schedule's all arranged. I've bought my ticket to Ft. Lauderdale. I just had my hair done. Oooh! I can't believe he would stand me up this way. And go off like that."

"One time when Alex and I had our sailboat in New York, he tried to treat me that way," Frances said. "So I just disappeared for a few days, went to a boutique dermatologist and had a face lift. Then I checked in at the Ritz-Carlton and had one of those fancy coif hairdos. Shopped 'til I maxed out his Discover Card." She laughed. "He had the whole New York police force out looking for me and everything."

"Frances! Did you really?"

"It was a real hoot, Mary. Fabulous. And you can bet Alex has been a little more attentive and obliging since then."

Mary sighed and looked at her cards. "I'm sorry, where were we?"

"I bid four hearts. I'm telling you, Mary, shoot Joe in the foot if he pulls that kind of stuff."

"Even that might not be enough," she managed a laugh and looked at her hand. "Five diamonds."

"I should double, but I'll let you by this time." Frances led a low club. Mary reached across to her dummy hand and followed suit with a jack. Frances played the queen, Mary played the three, letting Frances' dummy hand win the trick.

"Where's he going? Some dangerous place with lots of spies and murderers and gangsters and all kinds of exciting people, I imagine." Frances looked up. "Oh, I didn't mean to worry you about all that, dear. He just seems to have some penchant for that sort of thing, you know. So, what hair-raising adventure is it this time?"

"Oh, some boating job somewhere. Your lead."

Frances led her king of spades from the table. "It's hard to get that boating business out of their systems. Goodness knows, Alex is off in Charleston still seeing to repairs on our boat. He probably wants to drag me off on another sailing trip to who knows where. And I'll go, of course."

Mary played the ace and took the trick. "I thought you liked sailing." She led the queen of diamonds.

"Actually, I usually like sailing if it's calm and we end up in some nice marina with a good restaurant nearby." Frances sloughed the five. "I have to keep an eye on Alex though. He's always finding some young little chick for me to chase away. You're lucky if Joe behaves himself."

Mary sighed. "I hope so," she said and led the ace of diamonds. She tried to focus on the game but was too preoccupied. There had been so much about Joe's mission in Northern Ireland that she did not know about. Even while he was at her home convalescing from the bullet wound in his shoulder, he hadn't talked much, claiming that he was duty-bound to secrecy.

"He makes me so mad!" Mary blurted without realizing it. "Oh, excuse me, Frances. I was just thinking of..."

"That sorry old Joe, of course," Frances said. "Get him off your mind, dear." She rearranged her hand. "You should go somewhere yourself. Take a vacation without him or something. Have your own fling." She sluffed the three.

Mary glanced at her opponent, letting the vacation notion sink in. "Maybe I'll just do just that." Mary blinked and looked at her cards. "Oh, let's see. Did I take that trick in my hand?"

"Yes, and I'll bet you meant to be on the board." Frances laid down her cards. "Never mind, I've got you set."

"I concede. Sorry, I'm just too upset to play." She watched Frances collect the cards and shuffle them.

"About that idea of a trip. You do need one," Frances said. "Fact of the matter is, I need one, too," She began warming to the notion.

"Let's just haul off and go somewhere together. We'll show those men what for."

Mary paused. A trip with Frances? Her first reaction was to be leery. But then... She took a swig of her gin and tonic and glanced at her rather zany friend. Yes, if you want excitement, she thought, go with Frances.

"Where would we go?" she asked. "Overseas?"

"Not Europe. Oh, hell no," Frances replied. "Paris to Palermo, Belfast to Budapest—been there, seen it all, my dear. Besides, I only have about ten days before Alex gets back and we have a wedding to attend. Let's go somewhere closer. Anything but the Bahamas, for gosh sakes."

"Mexico? Cozumel maybe, or San Miguel?" Even as she suggested those places, Mary realized they were too tame and touristy.

"No, we want something more exotic," Frances said.

Mary took up her iPhone and scanned. A pop-up ad caught her attention.

THERE HAS NEVER BEEN A BETTER TIME TO TRAVEL TO CUBA.

Mary stared at the statement and then read it aloud to Frances.

"Oh yes, Cuba!" Frances lit up and nearly bolted to a magazine on her coffee table. She thumbed through. "Funny, I came across this the other day." She brought the magazine over and plopped it on the card table, pointing to a full-page ad with the headline, *VEN A CUBA!*

"Come to Havana for fun and excitement," she read aloud. "There's never been a better time to visit our beautiful island!"

"Except it is a communist country. I don't know. Do you think it's safe?"

"Oh pooh!" Frances replied. We can take a stick to beat off all the commies. I have a pistol. Of course, Alex keeps hiding it from me. I don't know why. I suppose he thinks I'll shoot him one night when he gets home later than he should. You've got to keep these men in line, know what I mean?" Mary had tuned her out and was continuing to search on her cell.

"Here's something about, 'there are ways to travel legally to Cuba?' Some sort of new regulations? What does that mean?"

"A few months ago, the Jemisons went to Cuba," Frances replied. "They came back raving about what fun it was. Of course, I can't imagine that really—being so friendly with the Russians. Better dead than red we used to say."

"Cuba might be different," Mary interrupted. "It's uh…well, not exactly exotic, but it is communist, and would be somewhat forbidding or something." It might not equal Joe's kind of CIA missions, dammit, she decided, but at least she wouldn't be at home fuming over his having left her.

"This says, "The United States government has tightened its rules about traveling to Cuba." Mary read aloud. "What's this about 'tightening rules?' I thought Cuba had just thrown out the welcome mat to us." She surfed to another website.

"'You can still go,' this says. *Still go?* What's that all about?" She read further. "The American government, as part of its ongoing economic embargo of Cuba's socialist government, announced on June 5th new rules for Americans traveling to Cuba, which included a ban on cruise ships. "

"Embargo!" Frances said. "It's that old soandso! Just throwing his weight around, I suppose. What does he think he is—King of the World, or something? Did you say "new rules?" What new rules?" Mary clicked on the link.

"The Treasury Department said it would crack down on the most popular ways for Americans to visit the island," she read. "Yes, we can still go, but you're supposed to take one of these tours."

"Ha!" Frances smiled wickedly. "Mary, Mary. Don't you see? We have to go."

Mary took in a deep breath and gazed at her prospective companion. "Oh, why not?" she all but shouted. "Hell, yes, Frances! Let's go to Cuba!"

"Oh, good, I like your enthusiasm," Frances said, rubbing her hands together. "When Alex finds out I've gone to Cuba, he'll have a fit." She smiled impishly. "Yes, I like it."

Mary was looking up *visit Cuba*. "Here's a tour," Mary replied with uncontained, malicious excitement. "It's supposed to be a sort of an educational tour or something."

Mary read on. "Here's one you go on. You fly to uh, *La Habana* and then you join up with a tour group. Sounds highly regulated."

"Oh, bull! Rules are for children; don't you agree? And maybe for most people, I suppose, but not for two adventuresome women like us, who are out to show their husbands a thing or two. Well, Joe's not your husband, though he ought to be." She took up her own iPhone. "Here, what's the number for that travel agency?"

Mary gave her the phone number and watched her friend punch it in. In a few moments, Frances frowned.

"What is all this foolishness about?" She took the phone from her ear, tapped a digit and looked at Mary. "It said, 'if you'd like to speak to customer service, please press one'? If I didn't want to speak to customer service, I wouldn't have called in the first place. Besides, whoever heard of a customer service that ever offered any service?" She pursed her lips in disgust.

"Hello? We want to sign up for your cruise to Havana. Yes, the next one, the one that leaves…"

"Tomorrow afternoon," Mary said, frowning, realizing it was too late to go on that one.

"The twenty-fourth, that's right. Of July, of course. You do know this is July twenty-third, right? You sound Indian—Hindu and all that. Where are you? Never mind. What? You say it's all booked up? That doesn't matter. Just put me down. Two of us, I mean. What? Of course, you can. Just put your mind to it. Now look here, I know you're probably in Calcutta or New Delhi or God knows where, so you could not know much about what's going on with this tour thing. Why you're not even in the same global hemisphere as Cuba. Listen, did you know that our president—some people say they don't have any respect for our crude, loudmouthed, ignorant president, but I think he's a fine man. Don't you? I said, don't you think he's a fine man? He's a global leader; well, he thinks so, anyway. And don't you know about our former president, who was trying to reestablish relations between the United States and Cuba? Say, are you not in favor of what he was doing? You're a little dark-skinned yourself, aren't you? Of course you are, being over there in New Delhi or wherever. So shouldn't you be in support of our president? By the way, what is your name? Patel, I'll bet. What? Narithool? Okay, Mr. Narithool, put Mary and me down for that tour so that it won't appear as if you are trying to thwart all these wonderful efforts at foreign relations being made by our first black president, who sought to open the paths of love and friendship between two nations only ninety miles apart. And why should you, being thousands of miles away, want to impede our struggle to reunite two neighboring nations in peace and harmony? What did you say? Why, certainly it all hinges on our going on your tour tomorrow. What? You want me to hold? All right, but just for a minute, my dear Mr. Narrowpool—that was your name, narrow pool?"

While Frances was holding, she looked at Mary and shook her

head. "I don't know what the world's coming to—dealing with these foreign people over the phone when it all concerns something so clearly a home issue right here in America."

"What is that? Yes, Mr. Narrowpool, tomorrow. You can arrange it? I knew you were a swami or something. And certainly you didn't want to interfere with international relations. Hold on, let me get my credit card number. Don't go away, now." She put the phone down, found her wallet and pulled out a card. "Here it is—an American Express—My country 'tis of thee and all that. And don't you worry. My husband, Alex, has so much money to cover all the charges. He has money stuck away in all kinds of world banks—probably has some there in New Delhi or whatever place you're in. The number? Okay. You got a pen handy—probably made in China just like our pens. Ready?"

"Four five nine three…" She read off the numbers and so on. "You're such a dear, Mr. Narrowpool. Next time you come to Birmingham, you give me a call, Okay? I'll see that Alex takes you to lunch at The Club or something. Yes, you can send me an email confirmation. You've been such a fine fellow. No, there's absolutely nothing more you can help me with, you dear sweet thing. Goodbye now."

She put down the phone and smiled at Mary. "Getting what you want is all in how you talk to them, you see." Frances hardly took a breath. "Come on, let's go decide what clothes and things we're going to pack." She stood and clapped her hands. "Oh, boy, this is going to be so much fun!"

· CHAPTER THREE ·

I n spite of lightning and a line of thunderheads to the east, it was a beautiful night for crossing the Straits of Florida. Bright moonlight shone in the foamy windswept tops, cascading down the crest of three-foot swells. Struggling to maintain twenty knots, the aging forty-foot Hatteras sport fishing boat yawed and pounded in a moderate chop on its southwesterly heading. Its faded marine blue color blended in with the night sea. The captain, Fernando Ricardo, and his surly companion, Chacko, made a living delivering illegals from Cuba to Florida, Joe learned, and he hoped this experienced *contrabbandiere di immigrati* could get him and his so-called "crack" engineer companion ashore undetected.

Heinrich Heinz, the engineer from the Caterpillar factory in Kiel, Germany, supposedly was a hot-shot mechanic, more than qualified to run the impounded ship's engine and, therefore, the perfect companion to assist Joe on the mission. So far, however, Joe was not encouraged. The young German, a top-notch engineer by his own appellation, had spent most of the trip leaning over the side of Ricardo's boat vomiting into the waves.

A little chilly in his short sleeves because of the night breeze, Joe stood not far behind the helm, leaning on the exposed extra 500-gallon diesel tank, casually keeping an eye on the thin Cuban-American boat captain whose leathery brown skin looked as weathered as his boat.

"You may have a squall to go through on your trip back," Joe said, motioning toward the west.

"*Si, Señor*" Captain Fernando Ricardo replied with a shrug, keeping his attention on the compass course. Ever since they departed Key West at sundown, Ricardo had not spoken five sentences. In Ricardo's sort of business, Joe imagined, you didn't want to talk much to strangers. Heinz raised himself up and staggered over to them.

"How much longer," he asked, as he wiped his face with a towel.

Ricardo pointed to the southern horizon. "There's the glow of lights from Havana." He looked at his watch and made a quick calculation. "We should be at our destination in an hour or so." In response, Heinz groaned. Joe took him by the arm and led him to where they sat in the fishing chairs.

"Such a long way." Heinz said.

"Just try to calm down a bit, guy," Joe encouraged. "Nerves may be what's making you sick."

"I've never done anything like this before," Heinz admitted.

"Yeah, well, just do what I tell you and maybe we'll both survive."

"Survive? What do you mean? They told me I would just go to start the engine, that's all."

"Is that what they told you? Jesus, I got news for you, Heinrich. It may be a little more complicated than that."

"Will we be...?"

"Did they not tell you about the ship being under guard? Men with real guns looking for any excuse to shoot anybody who might want to take the ship away from them. Listen, they'd love to..." Joe paused. Even in the dark, he could make out the German's look of alarm. "Look, Heinrich," he said. "Just stick with me; do what I say, and we'll both get through this, all right?"

But Heinz, with his hand over his mouth, already was staggering back to the side of the boat.

Joe shook his head and turned to Ricardo.

"Where do we go ashore, *Capitán*?

"To the west of Havana, near Nuevo Mariel," he replied. "Many coast patrols lately, even helos, unfortunately. But my brother, Hosea, has chosen a secluded spot for us. Not to worry, *Señor*."

Joe grinned and jabbed his thumb toward Heinz, who was draped over the gunwale again, retching. "Tell him that, would you?"

• • •

IT WAS A LITTLE AFTER 0300 when the Hatteras slowed to idle about a half mile offshore. Without the roar of the engine, they now could hear the surf pounding the beach, and Joe's pulse quickened.

"We are heading into the Playas Banes, west of the town of Caimito. Normally, I go into a small inlet, but the tide is too low tonight."

"You mean we can't go in?" Heinrich asked.

"No worry, *Señor*. We go up to the beach, and you get off there."

"I, …I don't understand," Heinrich stuttered.

"*Facil, Señor*. I drop you out in four feet of water, and you wade ashore."

"You mean there's no pier or anything? We get in the water in the *nacht*?" Heinrich asked. "What about sharks?"

"*No hay problema*," Ricardo replied. "But there may be a few stingrays," he added with a wink at Joe.

Even though he had his own concerns, Joe had to grin at the German's wide-eyed expression. "So the idea is that we wade into shore on a beach we've never seen before, walk up to your brother's vehicle soaking wet, and drive into Havana just about dawn with almost no equipment or dry clothes. I guess my old friend Adams dreamed this one up."

"Not to worry, *Señor*," Fernando repeated, shaking his head. "Hosea will be there with his truck and perhaps some dry towels. He is most trustworthy and clever. You will be well taken care of."

After glancing at Heinz' worried expression and sighing with mild disgust, Joe stared into the twilight gloom, just able to make out the line of the sandy beach. The onshore breeze had created three-foot high breakers and likely some undertow current. Getting ashore would not be pleasant.

"How do you see what you're doing?" Heinrich asked, his voice quivering into falsetto.

"I have been in here many times, *Giovanotto*," Fernando replied. His engine at idle speed, he headed in closer, noting the readings on his depth finder. "We may not get any closer than about thirty yards."

Joe glanced at Heinz, who had a white-knuckled grip on the gunwale and hoped the German could swim if he had to. Gazing at the beach, he saw movement. Dark figures began to emerge from the sand dunes, making their way down and across the beach. He nudged the captain. "Uh oh, we have company."

"My return passengers, no?" the Cuban said.

"What? There was nothing said about passengers." Joe wheeled around at him. "This was supposed to be entirely secret." He was mad enough to deck him.

"We are discovered," Heinz wailed. "It's all failed. What shall we do?"

"Relax, *mi amigos*," the captain grinned. "No one ashore knows anything about your arrival, except my brother Hosea, of course."

"Does CIA know you're smuggling these people?"

"I don't ask why they have me bring you here. They don't ask why I bring my countrymen to Florida. *Entender?*"

Joe shrugged. It did make sense. And why shouldn't Ricardo be making his trip count for double pay. It was just good business, after all. "I still would have been happier if you'd told me ahead of time." He looked at Heinz for agreement. Instead, all he saw was an ashen face. It was clear that this German hotshot had no nerve.

Fernando slowed the engine again. As the Hatteras rolled in the surf, he told Chacho to get off his ass and go forward to ready the anchor. The boat rolled heavily as he turned the bow to seaward and called for the anchor to be dropped. Once the rode ran out enough to make the anchor hold, Chacko cleated the line, and the stern of the boat settled about twenty-five yards from the beach. The waves jerked the boat around as the anchor dug in, causing Joe to grab a handhold. Heinz stumbled and fell on the deck with a grunt. Joe sighed, offered him a hand up and glanced disgustedly at Ricardo.

In the pre-dawn first light, Joe could see the immigrants wading toward them. He motioned at Heinz to grab his gear. With reluctance the German picked up his backpack that contained a few important tools and a change of clothes. Joe's pack held a change of clothes, a chart of Havana harbor, a fake Canadian passport, and a lot of cash, both U.S. and Cuban. It also contained a Glock pistol with several loaded clips. Joe had complained to Adams that to be found carrying even a small pistol would get them into trouble they couldn't talk themselves out of. Adams, in his typical style, had nixed that idea.

"We want you to be able to shoot Heinz when you need to," Adams had replied with a chuckle. "Or yourself too, if the Cubans catch you."

"And you're lucky I don't have it with me right now," Joe told him, or CIA might have one less handler."

With that thought, Joe shouldered his pack and asked the captain. "How will I recognize this brother of yours?"

"Not to worry, *Señor*, Hosea will find you. Good luck on your venture."

Joe nodded and looked at Heinz, who was puffing hard as if he had climbed the Matterhorn. "Okay, let's go."

Leading the way, Joe sat on the stern, which was equipped with a pass-through door to a swim platform. He waited for a big roller to pass underneath, took a deep breath, and slipped into the dark water. It was cold and up nearly to his chest. His feet found a sandy bottom. Shivering as much from nerves as from the nighttime chill of the water, he tried to hold his backpack above his head, but the waves made it impossible to keep good footing. There was some comfort in having the Cubans approaching from the beach.

Silently, they passed each other. Joe could make out the expressions of excitement, hope and dread in their faces. As many as ten men and women had passed him, fighting the surf as they made for the boat. At the end of the line was a young mother who was tugging on the arms of a screaming little girl, trying to force her toward the boat. A wave struck them, and the daughter strangled on a mouthful of seawater. She convulsed in sobs and coughs, but her mother kept tugging frantically, pulling her deeper. Slinging his pack over his left shoulder, Joe waded to them and picked up the girl, who coughed again, kicked, and screamed.

"Let me help," he said. "*Te ayudo, uh, Déjame ayudarte.*" The mother tried for a second to pull the girl away, then relented. Joe stumbled back to the pitching boat and handed the child to outstretched arms. He grabbed the mother by the wrist as the boat heaved in the waves and guided her up on the transom. Falling back, he regained his footing, pulled his pack strap back on his shoulder and again waded toward the beach. He ruefully realized that, along with everything else, he was helping—aiding and abetting—illegal immigrants.

Bracing himself against waves breaking on his backside, he waded ashore. The soft sand squinked under his soaked shoes. Joe looked around for his companion, but Heinz was not on the beach.

"Heinz?" he shouted. There was no sign of anyone heading his way. "Heinz," he called out louder. There was no reply. When all of the immigrants were aboard, the engine rumbled to life. Joe watched the boat begin moving slowly to sea. The first light of dawn was appearing in the east. As the anchor came up, the boat headed away, In the increased light, he could make out the blond head of Heinz amid the huddled group of black-haired passengers, not even looking his way.

"Heinz," Joe shouted. "You sorry, chicken-shit bastard." There went his only companion, the only one with a prayer of running the ship's engines. "Bloody hell!" he exclaimed and splashed on, running.. A silhouetted figure emerged from the dunes and walked up behind him.

"Welcome to Cuba, *señor*."

Joe turned to encounter a man wearing denim jeans and a brown polo shirt, smiling broadly. He motioned toward the departing boat.

"*¿Quien es usted?*" Joe demanded.

"I am Hosea, Fernando's brother and business partner."

"In the business of smuggling immigrants, I see." Joe said. He turned back to stare at the boat moving fast out to sea. He could just make out Heinz looking back at him.

"If I ever get my hands on that kraut, I'll kill that son of a bitch," he shouted.

"I see you have lost an *amigo,*" Hosea said. "But perhaps he was not the kind to share your fortunes, anyway."

Composing another epithet for Heinz, Joe paused listening. In the distance to the west was a staccato rumbling and the lights of an aircraft approaching down the beach.

"*Hola! Escuchar!* Patrol helo coming."

Both of them ran for the dunes. The Cuban nearly tackled Joe, pulling him down into the grass. The helo approached, slowed to a hover, and its pilot shinned a light where the immigrants had left footprints in the sand. It made a circle above the two men who lay in the saw grass and then made a wider circle out to sea. Joe looked up to spot the boat, but it was lost in the gloom. Finally, the helo resumed its path travelling east down the beach. A hand gripped Joe's elbow to pull him up.

"Did they see the boat?"

"I don't know," Hosea replied. "What matters is, can Fernando run out beyond the twelve-mile limit before the helo can summon a nearby patrol boat?"

"What happens if he doesn't?"

"We all will be in *mierda honda* if they catch him." He sighed. "*Que sera' sera'.*" He picked up Joe's pack and handed it to him. "So I drive you to Havana, no?"

Joe nodded. "*Dirige el camino, amigo.* Just lead the way."

"This way, *amigo, de prisa.* We must hurry."

CHAPTER FOUR

On the way to Havana with Hosea, Joe watched an orange sun rise over the distant mountains to the southeast, soon creating a blinding glare through the windshield of the 1955 Ford 150 pickup. The warmth was helping dry out his damp, salty clothes, at least, and his backpack seemed to have survived the wade in through the surf.

Damn that sorry Heinz!

He resolved to forget about him. There were a lot of other issues to occupy his mind, not the least of which was where he would find an engineer. He would have phoned CIA immediately to report Heinz's defection, but Adams had warned him to use the phone sparingly, and not anywhere except in the crowded city. Only among a lot of people could he hide his exact location in the event the phone signal was detected by Cuban electronic intelligence. As the truck bounced through potholes, Joe worried about how much he could trust this driver beside him.

Being Fernando's brother, however, Joe decided, there was little doubt Hosea Ricardo was a criminal type. But then whose law was he breaking?

The Castro government likely was unhappy about his recruiting Cubans for immigration to Florida. And he was abetting his brother in the violation of immigration laws of the United States. Such a man as this was not someone in whom to trust your fate, Joe decided.

"What brings you to Cuba, *señor*?" Hosea broke the silence. "After some evil communists, I think."

"Just heading to the docks. I have some business there, that's all."

"Forgive me, *señor*. We Cubans are curious. Prying is our favorite pastime." A boar ran out of the palmetto undergrowth and crossed the road. Nonchalantly, Hosea swerved to avoid it. The springs of the old truck groaned as it careened but steadied and moved on.

"And your name is Joe? Joe what?"

"Just *Joe* will do, okay?" Joe said, a bit irritated by the man's familiar, persistent, prying manner. "And I simply will call you Jose'."

"I am Hosea, *ho-say-a*h, like the the prophet of the Old Testament. My mother loved to read the Bible—very unusual for Catholics," the Cuban said and gave Joe an appraising glance. "And so, you must be Joseph with the coat of many colors—*si*, many colors--fitting for a spy."

Joe shifted uncomfortably in his seat. "Look, Hosea," he said, "if we are to get along, you need to shut up about the spy stuff. You got me?"

"Entiendo, mi amigo," Hosea laughed. "You don't say I'm a smuggler. I don't say you're a spy who has just invaded my country. Agreed?"

Joe gave a tentative nod.

Hosea smiled. He reached over and slapped Joe on the knee. "Not to worry, *amigo*. You have something on me. I have something on you. We both are outside the law. It makes us *compadres*, no?"

"Si, bueno," Joe replied, attempting amiability. *"Mi compadre."* What he thought, however, was that this hombre might just deliver him to the police and maybe get a reward. And how would he stop him? Adams would maintain that killing him was an alternative to consider. It was either that or just trust him. Joe glanced at the swarthy Cuban with long flowing sideburns, a handlebar moustache and a scar down his neck who did not inspire much trust. Uneasily, he tried to sit back and enjoy the bumpy ride.

After another few miles, they left the coastal plain. The road climbed a low ridge and then settled in a valley running east. A small village lay between acre-sized fields of what looked like corn but on second look appeared to be tobacco growing. A dirt road ran to the right from the highway toward the village. Without comment, Hosea slowed and turned. Joe sat up surprised and eyed the driver suspiciously.

"I need to visit some people for a few moments," Hosea explained. "It will not take long."

"You didn't say anything about stopping," Joe protested. Maybe there was a police station there, he imagined, and then what? Hosea shook his head gently as if he knew Joe's thoughts.

"Look, *Señor* Joe. You can relax. Please stop your worry. These *Peones* will have coffee for you and perhaps a bite to eat."

Joe gritted his teeth and then sighed. Although he was anxious to get to Havana and get away from this character, there was no timetable after all. So why not just take it easy?

In front of a low shack of a building with a corrugated rusting steel roof, three men in work clothes sat outside. They ceased talking and watched silently as Hosea stopped the truck and got out. Nervously, Joe watched as Hosea walked over to speak. Scrawled on the side of the building in white paint was the word *CAFÉ,* with a dripline of paint running off the bottom of the *F.*

Given a moment alone, Joe quickly unzipped the upper pocket of his pack, pulled out the Glock pistol and ankle holster. He wiped the seawater off, inspected the action, inserted a loaded clip, snapped it into the holster and strapped it to his ankle. Taking a deep breath, he got out of the truck and walked over to where Hosea was greeting several men. Hosea motioned at Joe, said something Joe couldn't quite hear, and the Cubans laughed. Hosea waved Joe to come on, and the whole group followed them inside.

Dim light beamed in from small windows, revealing benches, rough tables, and upside- down nail kegs for furniture. Two women in faded red blouses and grey skirts behind a bar were busy preparing food, using a wood stove with a big copper pot and a black cast iron frying pan.

Several groups of men and women sat at tables and waved at Hosea, whose arrival apparently was expected. All eyes, however, were on Joe. Hosea gestured grandly at him.

"*Aqui hay una señor Joe recién llegada de Florida,*" he announced, "*esta misma mañana.*" Joe was shocked.

"Hosea, shut up, dammit!"

"Oh, they do not care why you are here," Hosea laughed. "Don't worry. To them you merely are proof as to how close Miami is."

• • •

WITH A MAGNANIMOUS FLOURISH, Hosea ordered for everyone coffee and whatever kind of breakfast tortillas were available. Feeling like someone caught without his pants, Joe followed him to a table and sat. A woman brought coffee in an assortment of cups and porcelain mugs for everyone. Another brought around tortillas dripping in sorghum, and Joe fell to as if he hadn't eaten in days.

"In thankfulness for your safe passage to our island, *Señor,*" Hosea said with a grin, "perhaps you should treat."

Joe should have seen that coming. Good naturedly, he pulled out a few damp CIA-supplied pesos from his pocket and laid them on the table. The coffee was very good, he discovered, just exactly what he needed after the hard night at sea and the wade in through the waves. His clothes were mostly dry now, and he was becoming a bit more comfortable. Hosea drank a few swallows from his cup and then stood up.

"*Buenos días, amigos,*" he said. Waving everyone in the room to come over, he continued in Spanish. "I have something to tell you, my friends. I am your passport to freedom. You have heard of me. I, Hosea, am the one who can deliver you to the United States."

To Joe's surprise there was only a slight stirring and then a kind of dead silence as if the people barely could allow themselves such hope. Hosea pressed on with a broad smile.

"*Mi amigo, Señor* Joe, here," Hosea bowed his head slightly to indicate the now highly agitated Joe, who would have preferred total anonymity.

"My brother brought him in his boat," Hosea went on. "We do not ask why he is here. He is only proof that Florida is so very close. After my brother brought him to Cuba, he then left for Miami with about fifteen of your *compadres* from another village. They are bound for a new life and new riches in the land of your dreams." He looked at his watch. "They will be in Miami before the sun goes down. You, *mi amigos*, could make the next trip." There was a silence as Hosea let the idea sink in. Then as Joe sat there feeling rather naked, one man stood up. Likely in his forties, Joe guessed, the man appeared to have just come in from working in the field in the early morning, already dirty and tired, but with a glint of excitement in his eye.

"*Cuánto?*" he asked. "*Cuánto cuesta por un famile?*"

"Five hundred pesos a head for adults, two hundred for each child, babes in arms nothing."

The farmer did a mental calculation, shook his head sadly, and sat down. There were murmurs among the others. One of the women came over to the farmer, leaned over his shoulder and whispered in his ear. Joe could see a kind of desperate excitement in her eyes, but the man just shook his head. She closed her eyes, and when she opened them, a tear ran down her cheek. Another man spoke. "Must we pay all at once? That is many pesos for poor farmers like us. The crops will be lean this year. Can we pay half and then the rest over time in America?"

"No, *señor*," Hosea said. "Once you arrive in Florida, we cannot ever see you again."

The man looked at Joe. "And how do we fare, *Señor* Joe? What happens to us when we get to your country?"

Joe stared in surprise. "Hold on. I'm a Canadian."

Hosea smirked. "Oh, yes, and I'm Yugoslavian, or a monkey's uncle from Uganda."

Joe gave him a hard look. "I don't have anything to do with this. This is all between you and Hosea."

"Then why are you here?" the first man asked. Joe looked at him and then glanced at Hosea, who just smiled back.

"What he does is not our concern," Hosea said. "Look my friends," I will come by again soon. You can tell me then if you wish passage to America. And bring your pesos, Comrades." With that he nodded to Joe that they should leave. Joe gulped the last of the coffee, put another five pesos on the counter and jumped up to follow, conscious of the inquisitive Cubans staring at his back.

Without a word they both climbed in the truck, and Hosea drove back up the dirt road, turned east on the highway and headed on toward Havana.

"Hosea," Joe said, with all the restraint he could muster, "Do you realize you really compromised me. Now that whole town knows I am here and that I got here on your brother's boat, illegally."

Hosea glanced over at him and laughed. "Do you think they would tell the police anything? *No, mi amigo espia.* They all want out of Cuba. And they know not to say a word about me or you. If I am found out, they will lose their chance to go. You are safe because I am safe, I assure you."

Accepting that assurance with the thought, *what else can I do*, Joe thought about the immigration problem.

"How many Cubans have you and your brother taken to the States?" he asked.

"Hundreds, thousands," Hosea replied proudly. "Who knows?"

"I suppose you think of yourself as doing some good for your people," Joe guessed. "But what about building this country? Don't you think it would be better if the Cuban government helped these poor people so they could stay home and have better lives here?" Hosea cut his eyes around and gave Joe a look of amusement.

"Better lives, *Señor*?" he said. "Better lives for the poor?" He looked at the road and corrected his steering. "If a *choncholi* bird lays an egg and the fox comes to eat it, then she merely lays another, and then another. Poor people live on the edge, my amigo, just like the birds and the animals. Their numbers are limited only by hardship, by poverty or violence or murder. It is the rule that if life can exist, it will exist until conditions become too harsh for life to go on. When we take people to Florida, some will make it there and some may starve and die. But here in Cuba, they will be replaced by those who are left behind. It is the rule of nature."

"That's pretty cynical," Joe said. He vividly recalled the frightened little girl he carried through the surf, her brown eyes wide with fright. "So you don't care what happens to the people? You just take their money and send them on their way?"

"And *viejo diablo* shall take the hindmost. Isn't that what they say?"

Joe regarded this Cuban whom he had known for only a couple of hours, realizing that he had met up with, not a hero and savior, but only a pied piper of hope, who took the life savings of peasants, sending them to America to make of it what they can.

"You're a hard man, Hosea," he said. Hosea smiled thinly and shrugged.

"Who does more for them than I? But one can do just so much." Hosea was interrupted by his cell phone ringing. "I didn't think I could receive a signal out here," he remarked as he answered.

"Fernando? Is that you? I can barely hear. Como? No!" Hosea listened for twenty seconds and slammed on the brakes, stopping in the road. *"Mierde! Marina de Guerra... Como ocurrio? Allo* Fernando? Fernando?" Joe looked at Hosea who had turned pale. He took the phone from his ear and sat motionless, staring out the windshield.

"What happened?" Joe asked.

"Fernando has been captured! The patrol."

"Surely they made it out beyond the twelve-mile limit," Joe said.

"Engine overheated. They were just sitting when..." He looked at Joe. "He said they were being arrested by the Cuban Navy?"

"Si, si. Espantoso!" A horn blew loudly behind them. Then a truck loaded with sugarcane rumbled past. Hosea pulled over to the side of the road.

"With the immigrants aboard, and Heinz, too?" Joe asked.

"It is a calamity for all of us." Hosea shook his head sadly. "They will be interrogated harshly."

"And that damn Heinz will talk," Joe said through gritted teeth. "That spineless bastard will tell them everything." He banged his fist on the dashboard. "Come on, will ya. I've got to get to Havana.

Hosea threw up his hands in dismay, gunned the old truck, and headed east.

• • •

THEY CAME TO AN INTERSECTION of a larger highway with more traffic. Joe watched a '55 Chevy speed by, passing a 60's model Ford sedan. A Pontiac with V-shaped tail fins and a bad muffler rumbled by. It felt to Joe as if he had gone back in time. Hosea gunned the truck onto the highway, continuing generally eastward. Joe could make out buildings in the distance.

"Habana," Hosea said, gesturing at the distant buildings. Joe nodded as the sight caused him a sudden stab in the gut. He now had

two immediate problems. The first was to separate from Hosea without giving the man any knowledge of where he was going. And the second was to find some kind of engine mechanic. If he could accomplish those goals, then just maybe he could tackle the huge problem of taking the ship. All of it would have to be achieved before Heinz gave in to police interrogation and revealed the entire plot. This damn mission, he thought, was becoming even more impossible.

CHAPTER FIVE

With a line of impatient passengers behind them, Mary stood beside Frances at the American Airlines counter, the kiosk robot not having found their reservations.

"Of course we have reservations, dear man," Frances said. "We booked them last night. You have a tour group leaving for Havana at 8:15 this morning. Here we are, all ready to go."

The thirty-year old agent, who looked to Mary as if he had just graduated from ticketing-agent school, rekeyed his computer and looked up at them.

"I have no reservation for either a Frances Smith or a Mary Johnston, ma'am. Besides, it's too near to boarding time..."

"Don't be silly," Frances cut him off. "I phoned last night and spoke to Mr. Narrowpool—Naitool, or something like that—a nice Indian man, Hindu most likely, in Calcutta or Delhi or God knows where. At first, he said he couldn't get us on the tour, but he did it by the time I finished talking to him. I explained how we needed to improve relations with Cuba, don't you see? And we need a new people-to-people program. A great idea, don't you agree, Mr. uh... McGuire is it? Mr. Narrowtool thought it was a wonderful idea. You don't want to stand in the way of improving international relations, do you, even if it is with a pinko communist country? No, I didn't think you did." She thrust her credit card across the counter. "So here's my husband's VISA card. He's so rich he's probably on the board of your airline." She leaned toward him with a serious look. "He oversees the hiring and firing of ticket agents, Alex does. Imagine that!" She waved the plastic card at him. "So go ahead and punch all those nice numbers into your computer thing there and give us our tickets. This is such an important moment in the relations between Cuba and our own wonderful country. Just imagine what an important job you have putting us on this flight!"

Frances looked back over her shoulder at the impatient people waiting in line.

"I apologize for this agent's inefficency," she whispered to them. "He's young, as you can see, and still learning his job. We should be patient and nice to him."

Mary suppressed a laugh. As anxious as she was becoming, it was fun watching her friend in action. Frances continued to hold her arm outstretched, waving the credit card until he took it and began punching information into his terminal.

"Let me see what I can do. Just a minute please."

"Here are our bags right here," Frances went on. She threw hers on the scale. "Here Mary, hand me your bag. Let's just put both our tickets on Alex's card. You can pay me back sometime. We want to make things easy for our handsome and thoughtful agent, don't we, Mr. McGuire?"

"It does appear we have a couple of cancellations," the agent said. "Let me have your passports, please."

As they both dug into their purses for their passports, Frances whispered, "See, Mary, people can be very reasonable if you merely explain things properly."

· · ·

THE ONLY INSTRUCTION JOE had given Hosea was to go south of the bay, *Bahia de la Habana*, and turn left and go north on *Carretera Casablanca*. Hosea's old truck rattled its way into the city. People were everywhere, even in the hot salt-smelling, sticky humidity of a sunny July day. Street vendors hawked bright colored shirts and straw sombreros. They passed sidewalk markets with slabs of hogs' ribs swinging in the breeze, chickens with legs bound lying on their sides, men and women shouting their wares, laughing and boisterous. Joe had expected to find a quiet street, a secluded alley, anyplace where he could ask Hosea to let him out of the truck unseen. Obviously, with so many people around, it was impossible.

"When you get to the intersection with *Carretetera A Naval*, you can let me out there."

"*No hay problema*, Joe," Hosea assured him.

In heavy traffic of mainly trucks and sixty-year old automobiles, Hosea abruptly turned left, careening the truck to clear an oncoming bus.

"Take it easy, will ya," Joe commanded, and noted Hosea's impish grin. Shaking his head and taking a deep breath, Joe saw they were approaching commercial wharves. Ahead was a bright blue bay streaked with ripples from the westerly breeze. They drove between rows of warehouses, and beyond he could see a docked merchant ship with a tall crane unloading cargo. From the satellite photo Adams had shown him, this appeared to be the right area.

"Okay, Hosea, you can let me out here," Joe said. But Hosea kept going.

"We may as well ride by the ship, no?"

"Wait, what ship? Just stop here."

"Come now, Joseph, you should know I have guessed by now. You are here because of the American ship, of course."

"Son of a bitch! You're not supposed to know..."

"*Despacio, despacio, señor*. Why else would your government send you here?" Hosea drove on past the row of warehouses and onto the wide concrete commercial wharf. Beside a large freighter two ancient forklifts moved loaded pallets, which had been deposited on the dock by the ship's crane.

Passing several ships moored at the quay, Joe spotted a dark red hull with a white mast rising above the amidship superstructure. On its stern painted in faded white letters amid a few rust spots was the name *Sea Urchin*. At the sight of the ship, he felt a great rush of adrenalin. Hosea regarded him with a grin.

"*Mira ahi, ahi esta.* Your prize, yes?"

"Just drive on," Joe said, too awed by seeing the ship to be concerned with Hosea's accurate deduction. An aluminum gangway traversed the fifteen-foot drop from the ship's deck to the pier. Beneath a tan-colored canopy erected under the gangway, a uniformed soldier sat in a dilapidated chair with a rifle resting beside him. A yellow banner stretched across the gangway read, "*SIN ENTRADA.*"

"Seen enough?" Hosea asked. Joe nodded, and Hosea drove on. "There's a place to eat around the corner. I'll take you there."

Joe looked warily at the older man, realizing how much Hosea's knowledge of his mission made him a threat. Joe's training dictated neutralizing, even eliminating, such a person so as not to leave the mission in jeopardy. It was a terrible thought but something for Joe to consider. Hosea glanced at him and apparently read his thoughts. For an instant of recognition, they regarded one another with malice. Then Hosea laughed.

"We find ourselves in an interesting situation, eh, Joseph?" he said.

"Explain what you mean."

Hosea pulled the truck over to the curb and stopped. "With Fernando arrested by the coast patrol, along with your mechanic, who you say will be too gutless to stand up to interrogation, we—you and I—now share a common danger and therefore a common goal."

"And what is that exactly?" Joe asked warily.

"Let me just say that I need to help you take that ship away from here."

"Look," Joe said. "I don't know you well enough to trust you, *amigo*. The best thing we can do is say *adios* and then deal with our own problems. The sooner we go our separate ways, the better, understand?" Hosea raised his hands and gave a hurt look.

"You, a spy, a CIA agent, invading my country, do not trust me? I'm only an honest smuggler and human trafficker." He laughed again. "*Somos compadres, compadres en el crimen.*"

"I could argue the question about who is criminal," Joe replied. "Cuba took our ship illegally, so I..."

"And what is so important about that ship that they would send you here to steal it back?" Hosea grinned. "Never mind. That is not of my concern, *amigo*. I don't care why you wish to risk your life doing such a dangerous, *de hecho peligroso*. And I sure as hell don't know how you will do it." He threw up his hands in bewilderment. "But *es más importante,* I do know you must have an engineer. That is certain. So perhaps I can help find you one."

Joe silently considered the offer. God knows, he needed an engineer. But his instincts told him to separate from this character because Hosea knew too much.

"*Muchas gracias, amigo,*" Joe replied. "But I'll just go it alone. Just let me out here, and I'll say *hasta luego.*"

Hosea shrugged, shook his head and drove another block. He stopped in front of a warehouse with a sign reading CAFÉ MARINEROS.

"You will find a good meal here, *señor,*" Hosea said with some dejection. "Now, for the ride to town, you owe me $500.00, U.S. dollars, *por favor.*"

Joe stifled a reaction to such a price, opened his pack, and counted out the money. He handed it over, opened the door, took up his bag and got out. "Remember, Hosea, you never saw me."

The Cuban nodded. "We shall see," he said. "*Vaya con Dios, compadre. Hasta la vista.*"

Joe closed the door and watched until the old Ford pickup disappeared around the corner. *See you again? I sure as hell hope not.*

Just across from the cafe there was a narrow alley between warehouses. Joe walked into it, glanced to see that no one was around, and punched Adams' number into his phone.

"Joe, you're late," Adams said. "I expected to hear from you an hour ago."

"I'm late? Fuck that! Listen, do you have any idea what's happened? After I came ashore, Ricardo's boat was stopped by the Cuban coast patrol. And that ace mechanic of yours was arrested. The asshole wouldn't get off the damn boat."

"You mean he abandoned you?"

"Hell, yes. The chickenshit is probably spilling the whole plan to the police."

"What time did that happen?"

"Hell, I don't know. I heard about it an hour or so ago. Do you think I put a stopwatch on it?" He realized he was shouting, took a breath, and lowered his voice. "The question is, what are you gonna do about getting me a new engineer?"

"I'll get on it right away. In the meantime, try to find one there."

"Here? Oh sure. There's a Russian ship at the dock. I'm sure they have one I can hire. Damn!"

"Just calm down and think about it. Maybe you can do without..."

"Oh, that's crazy! Of course, I can't, you idiot." Joe realized he was yelling again.

"Why don't you see if you can get aboard the ship; take a look at the engine. Maybe there are some remote controls in the pilot house."

"Go aboard? Oh sure. Maybe the guard with the AK 47 is selling tour tickets."

"Okay, okay, I'll see what I can do. Meanwhile you'd better be looking around, too. And figure out how you can take out the guard."

"Take out? Shoot the guard? Of course, shoot the guard, walk aboard, start the engine and sail away. How brilliant; great CIA technique. Wish I had thought of it."

"Listen, Joe. You cannot afford to panic. Just give us a few hours to find you some help. Call back later today. And just take it easy."

"And you know what you can do." Joe ended the call, beat his fists on his thighs and tried to regain his cool. After a minute or so, he walked out of the alley and headed for the cafe down the street.

• • •

CAFÈ MARINEROS WAS NOT more than a corner space in a rambling old warehouse which looked as if the exterior had not been painted in decades. To either side of the front door there were metal mullioned windows with rust streaks running down the faded and dirty glass. Likely a greasy-spoon sort of place, he imagined, suitable only for dock workers and transient sailors. What he needed to do now was go in, have some lunch, and try to meld into the scene as just another merchant seaman from one of the ships in port. As he grabbed the door handle to pull it open, he took a deep breath and muttered, "Well, here goes."

The acrid smell of cigar smoke mixed with the odor of frying corn hit him as he entered. The interior looked like a cheap diner that could be found anywhere in America. Behind a low counter was a short order cook whose oily black hair hung over a sweaty white T-shirt. A waitress with short brown hair shouted an order to him in Spanish over the din of conversation in different languages and accents.

A dozen or so men in wrinkled soiled shirts, all needing haircuts and shaves, sat around at tables and in cushion-less wooden booths. With his now dried-out khaki pants and faded plaid shirt he fit in very well. The place was crowded and noisy, and nobody paid any attention to him, which was good.

The tables in every empty booth were covered with dirty dishes from the previous customers. Joe chose one near the back that was the least messy and took a seat. Pushing dishes to the other side of the table, he stole a look at the patrons.

Four men within hearing were speaking a Slavic language, Russian, most likely. One with a red beard that came to a sharp point must be named Ivan, he decided. The others were swarthy, and their faces had a windburned look. The biggest of them was mopping up gravy with a biscuit gripped in his meaty hand.

Across from them were three Hispanics and one black African. Two of the Hispanics wore red bandannas around their necks. The black man had huge biceps and gold loop earrings. They all had finished their meal and were smoking big Cuban cigars, hence the thick odor competing with grease smell. One swarthy-faced young man had a scar running down his neck, disappearing under his collar. He noticed Joe staring and stared back briefly before both looked away.

Joe pondered the motley gathering of seaman and tried to imagine their personalities. Like his great friend in Northern Ireland, Big Ryan, each man had chosen a life at sea for some personal reason. For Ryan, it had been to leave a family divided by religion, the Catholics intolerant of the Protestants and vice versa. One of the Russians, the one with sunken sad eyes, Joe guessed, may have been abused or beaten by his father. Another black man seated alone carried a boatswain's knife in a sheath at his waist and looked as if he'd pull it on you at the slightest provocation.

A pair of Nordic looking young men in their twenties sat in a corner booth. Joe noticed the way they looked at one another with a kind of doting deference and realized they likely were not only shipmates but lovers. He wondered if they kept to themselves because they were ostracized by the rest of their crew.

Each seaman likely had his own melancholy story. Going to sea offered not only adventure but an escape from having to measure up to whatever standard a father might have imposed. Or a wife may have driven them off. Joe personally knew something about that, having been married as a young man and soon divorced. Or a man might have served time in jail for a mistake he made as a youngster. Each man had run away from home, being a misfit in some way, Joe realized. And each had his own experience, unique in difficult circumstances and probable sadness.

He took one of the menus clad in cracked, greasy plastic and looked it over. It was written in both Spanish and English. Potatoes were featured as often as refried beans and tortillas to suit the tastes of merchant sailors from anywhere. He was trying to decide between ham and eggs or hamburger steak when the waitress came over.

"*Buenos dias,*" Joe said, appraising her, deciding she was in her forties.

"Hi ya, Mac," she replied, slopping in front of him a glass of water with no ice. Her Brooklyn accent surprised him, and he grinned.

"How's the hamburger steak?" he asked. She glanced toward the kitchen and leaned toward him.

"Wouldn't trust it, dear," she replied confidentially. "Couldn't swear it's beef, you know what I mean?" She winked and looked down at the menu. "I'd stick with the steak or pork or eggs if I was you. Now the Cuban omelet ain't bad 'cause I saw Rodolfo—he's the cook, Rodolfo is—I saw him cut up all the onions and peppers and stuff this morning. It wasn't all left out for the cucarachas to crawl over during the night, get it? Yeah, definitely go with something I can vouch for." She gave him a big wide smile, and Joe realized she was favoring him a bit. He ordered the omelet with fried potatoes and toast and coffee. While she was gathering up and precariously stacking the leftover dirty dishes, he decided to satisfy his curiosity.

"What's a pretty girl like you doing in a place like this?"

She grimaced. "It's a living, know what I mean."

"But how did you get to Cuba? I assume you've lived here a while." She stared at him skeptically for a moment with her brown eyes and then softened her gaze.

"Want to hear my sob story, huh? Well, in New York I met a guy off a ship and we kinda fell into it, know what I mean? And he convinced me to join the crew as a cook. His captain said okay and got me my papers. So I go with him on this ship—a real banana boat, let me tell you. Anyway, we come down here to Havana and have a fight all the way—I really misjudged the guy. So when we arrive in port, I jumped ship more or less and happened into this job here, and the government let me stay. Four years, now, and getting sick of the place, get it? But there ain't much to go home to. So here I am. Any more questions?"

"That's quite a story," Joe said. He was about to go on, but the cook was yelling at her.

"Marsha, *apúrate* Marsha."

She nodded and glanced at Joe. "Bring your order in a minute."

Joe watched her rush off with the dirty dishes, drop them with a clatter in a busing bin, wipe her hands on her apron and go to pick up the ready orders on the counter. He smiled as he thought of "Casablanca" and how this Mariners Cafe sure was a funny parody of Rick's.

When Marsha brought his food, she fussed over being sure he had ketchup or whatever else he might need. As he dug hungrily into the omelet, Joe noted the special attention and realized that, for whatever reason, he was making a friend. Perhaps she could be helpful.

"I'm looking for a diesel mechanic," he mentioned to her when she came around with his check. "Somebody who knows ship's engines. You wouldn't know anybody looking for that kind of job, would you?

"Nobody I know," she replied. "But I could ask around. Or you could put up a notice on the wall over there." She waved toward a space on the yellowed plaster where several papers were taped. Joe paused and then shook his head.

"I might get too many of the wrong kind of applicants," he said. "Better for me just to ask around." Advertising his need, he realized, was not feasible for an undercover agent. He stood, counted out pesos to pay the check and added a healthy tip. "Thanks. I'll check back with you later."

With a parting smile, Joe slung his pack over his shoulder and walked out. Once onto the street he headed toward the waterfront. He passed a couple of Hispanics walking toward the café—likely more sailors, he guessed. One nodded at him but neither paid him any attention. He did look like any other merchant mariner, and being from the States was not unusual, so there was no reason to think he didn't blend in. There were three old semis with flatbed trailers lined up facing the piers. A fourth was alongside a blue-hulled freighter, being loaded with grey CONEX boxes. The gantry crane creaked as it swung over the side of the ship to lower a box, and a man in a hardhat stood beside the truck, giving hand motions to the operator, directing the placement of a box. Another man in a yellow hardhat was yelling down a barrage of instructions in some dialect of Spanish or perhaps Portuguese that Joe couldn't understand. Likely from some South American country, he mused.

Joe reached the corner of the warehouse buildings and looked to his right. Another merchant ship, the one with a green hull, was moored about a hundred yards down the wharf. Across the stern in white letters, he could make out *OKEAHKNN MAPCOXOA* and in smaller letters VLADIVOSTOK. Clearly, the Russians continued their trade with Cuba.

The next ship moored to the quay was *SEA URCHIN*. The mere sight of it gave him goose bumps.

There seemed to be no activity. As casually as he could, he strolled past the Russian ship heading toward *Sea Urchin*. As he walked past the Russian ship, a salty warm breeze hit him, and he had to grab his cap to keep it from blowing off. Readjusting his pack, he walked closer to *Sea Urchin's* red hull, watching the mooring lines tighten and then ease as the wind blew against her broadside.

Midships was the aluminum gangway with about twenty steps up to the deck. It had a red banner across the entrance with a sign reading, "EN *CUARENTENA: NO HAY ENTRADA*."

Then he spotted the tarp canopy beneath the gangway. Under it was a chair, and in the chair was a guard, who looked to be in his twenties, wearing a somewhat rumpled blue uniform. Apparently, he was stationed there to enforce the quarantine. The man was leaning back with the chair on two legs, dozing peacefully. A somewhat outdated Kalashnikov AK 47 with a frayed web sling lay flat beside him. Noting the man's rumpled uniform and the frayed web shoulder strap on the rifle, Joe guessed that the Cuban military did not consider the ship worthy of their best spit-and-polish soldiers to guard it. Well, that was one good thing, anyway. Without pausing, Joe walked on by quietly, casually, as if merely out for exercise.

There was a long rust streak below a scupper, and several other patches of brown rust spotted the dark red hull. The white superstructure above the deck was badly in need of fresh paint as well. But the ship appeared to be floating high, the pimsoll mark two feet above the water. At CIA he had been told the ship was three hundred ten feet in length, not even as big as the guided missile frigate he had served aboard in the Navy. But without adequate crew, it would be more than a challenge to get it underway and negotiate the harbor passage to the sea. And then, of course, he still had no idea where he was going to get an engineer to run the big diesel that had been idle now for days.

Noting that there was no one watching, Joe turned around to walk back. As he passed the gangway again, he took in a deep breath, realizing that at some point he would have to climb those stairs, with or without anybody's permission—with or without someone pursuing him, with or without someone shooting at him from below. He shook his head.

"This is the craziest thing I've ever gotten into!" he said aloud. "It's as crazy as..." He paused, realizing that of past crazy things he had done, he had a choice as to which came closest to this.

• CHAPTER SIX •

The flight from Birmingham to Miami took two hours and fifteen minutes. and then they had to wait another two and half
hours for the flight to Havana which, once in the air after a forty-five
minute taxi and take-off, required only thirty minutes flying time. But
deplaning at *Aeropuerto Internacional José Martí, Habana* required an
additional twenty minutes.

As they wearily climbed the ramp into the arrival lobby, Frances
and Mary, along with two dozen other tourists were met by a young
Cuban woman in a gray uniform. With military efficiency, they were
herded to *INMIGRACIÓN* and then onto a bus where they waited
for the luggage. It took an hour for all the bags to be loaded and then
another hour through traffic to arrive at their hotel. Given another
two hours to register and check in to their rooms—Mary and Frances
shared a suite—the travel-weary pair were summoned to the tour bus
for an afternoon riding around Havana.

"Oh, not another church!" Frances complained loudly after an
hour of touring. She looked at Mary who sat beside her up front near
the driver and the standing tour guide. "Too many churches for a
communist country, don't you think?"

"Ladies and Gentlemen," the twenty-five year old guide said, "We
have arrived at *Catedral de la Virgin de la Concepcion Inmaculada de
la Habana,* built by Jesuits in 1727. A marvelous accomplishment in
architecture."

"Yeah," Frances said, "those busybody Jesuits probably made all the people go to confession and built this place on the offerings they made so they wouldn't go to hell or something. I'm glad I'm an Episcopalian. We're allowed all kinds of sins."

Mary put her hand on her companion's arm. "Frances, let the lady talk, please."

"Now we will go inside for a guided tour," the young woman continued. "Everyone remember, we must remain together at all times."

"Suppose we have to tinkle?" Frances asked. "Do we do that together, too?"

"We will allow time for necessities, *señora*," the mirthless guide replied.

"Well, you have laid out so many rules for us," Frances pressed. "I suppose you want to give us a taste of living under communism, huh? Say, *Señorita*, did you ever teach fourth grade? We Americans are accustomed to a bit more freedom, understand-dez?"

"We must abide by government regulations, *señora*. Now, everyone, this way, *por favor*."

Frances stood up. "Okay, I'll try to behave. Come on, everybody. Hurry, hurry!" As she made her way beside the bus driver, she glanced down at him.

"Juan, my dear man, *como speako* 'hurry'?"

The driver, a fiftyish man with a pot belly, grinned. "*De prisa. Muévete, damas y caballeros.*"

"Say, Juan," Frances replied. "You're kinda cute, too." She wiggled her shoulders at him, laughed, and stepped down to the pavement.

Mary paused as she went by the driver. "That's just her sense of humor. I hope you are not offended.

Juan grinned. "*Ella es como una cabra,*" he replied. "It's a Cuban expression for a very nice lady."

Mary nodded. She understood a little Spanish but was a bit

confused. As she got off the bus and passed the guide, she asked what the word, *cabra*, meant.

"Your word is *goat*, I believe."

A bit taken aback, Mary made no objection. In fact, watching Frances speaking something outrageous to an older couple in the group, Mary decided *cabra* might be a fitting appellation.

• • •

Several Cubans had come down to the wharf to fish. They stood between the ships to cast their lines. Joe was surprised to see they had caught a few—catfish mainly, but a few keepers as well. He struck up a conversation with one of the men and managed to buy his rod and reel by paying double its value. With his tackle in hand, Joe wandered down to the stern of *Sea Urchin*, cast the line out, and kept an eye on the guard at the gangway. The soldier on duty appeared to be an older man, who did not seem to mind sitting in the dilapidated chair for his entire watch. Tired of toting his backpack but not knowing what else to do with it, Joe slung it back on his shoulders, reeled in and moseyed over.

The guard, who was dozing with his rifle lying beside him, was plainly over seventy. His wrinkled uniform showed his loss of military bearing. As Joe approached, the man stirred and opened one eye.

"*Perdone, señor,*" Joe said. "I did not mean to wake you," he continued in Spanish. "Where might I catch a bus?"

The old man eyed him for a moment. "*¿El camión dónde tomo?*"

"To the other side of Havana and then back, I suppose," Joe said. "Just to see the sights?"

"*¿Americano?*"

"Canadian," Joe lied.

"*¿Navegante?*"

"*Sí,* but I am waiting for my ship to arrive. I have been on leave."

"How's the fishing?"

"No luck," Joe said, not mentioning he never had any bait on the hook.

"Try early in the morning," the guard said. "It's much better before it gets hot."

"Thanks for the advice. So you fish?"

"I used to fish when I was a boy. But not so much anymore." He stood up and stretched. Joe offered a handshake.

"*Me llamo Joe,*" he said with a smile. The old guard shook his hand with a surprisingly strong grip.

"*Soy Hermano.*"

"So why do you guard this ship, Hermano?" Joe ventured.

"It's an American ship. That's all I know. They never tell me, and I could care less."

"Just putting in your time, huh?"

"*Si, solo pongo mi tiempo,*" Hermano repeated wearily. "Four hours on duty, eight off. Sometimes day, sometimes night. *No hay fin para eso.* No end to it."

"I see. Well, I hope you enjoy your afternoon," Joe said. "*Hasta luego.*"

"*Chao pescao,*" Hermano said with a grin. Joe didn't know that expression, but he smiled back anyway. Something about a fish, maybe?

As the soldier settled back, crossed his arms, and closed his eyes, Joe strode on back toward the warehouses. One thing he had learned, the Cuban government was not so careful about guarding the ship they had impounded.

Now it was time to phone Adams again to see if that sorry organization had found him an engineer.

• • •

IN THE LATE AFTERNOON in front of the hotel, the tour weary crowd disembarked from the bus. They were surprised by a hoard of demonstrating

Cubans in front, protesting the poor economy, low wages, and food shortages. A few carried signs protesting the U.S. embargo, which was creating much of their hardship. The tourists were rushed inside to the lobby and given an apology by the tour guide.

"I am sorry for the disturbance. I know you are all ready to relax for a while. The bar is ready to serve you a cocktail."

"Oh yes," Frances announced, "a *Cuba Libre* in honor of those poor people out front. See what communism has done for them. What was that old saying? 'If you're red, you might as well be dead?'" She looked for applause, but obviously the *turistas* were too tired to react to Frances anymore.

"Thank you, Mrs. Smith," *Señora* Sara said in a thinly veiled voice of exasperation. "Dinner will be served in the Main Dining Room at 7:00. But remember please, we all must remain in the hotel until our tour tomorrow. The bus will arrive at 8:00 AM. Now enjoy your evening."

As the group dispersed, Mary started for the elevator, but Frances caught her arm.

"Let me show you something," she said, and led Mary to the window. "Did you notice that cute dress shop next door? Let's go check it out right quick."

"But Frances, we're supposed to stay in the hotel. Besides, I'm dog tired."

"Oh, come on, Mary. Where's your spirit? We came to have fun, not be herded around like school children. Look, there's a side entrance. We can slip out there."

Mary sighed. "Oh, why not? Let's go."

Once inside the little boutique, Mary was captivated by the colorful Cuban dresses. Frances picked one off the rack and held it up to her companion.

"This would look great on you!"

"In Havana, I suppose," Mary replied. "Though I wouldn't be caught dead in that thing back home, except maybe at Halloween or something."

With the help of a very pushy sales lady, and their own sense of mischief, they quickly tried on and bought the fanciest, frilliest, most colorful Cuban dresses and hats to go with them.

"Wait 'til I get home with this and show it to Alex," Frances laughed, "along with his credit card bill."

"I'd love to wear this outfit while we're here in Havana," Mary exclaimed.

Frances twirled to make her skirt fly. "Perhaps we'll find just the occasion, who knows?"

• CHAPTER SEVEN •

With Heinrich Heinz likely breaking under the harsh interrogation of Cuban authorities, Joe decided he'd better consider himself a wanted man. So, where could he spend the night? After an early supper at the café, he thought about going back to the little hotel he had passed a few blocks from the harbor. It seemed suitably shabby for transient sailors, and he was using a false sir name on his CIA-generated counterfeit Canadian passport. But an efficient police force would be reviewing the registers of all hotels, and they might have forced Heinz to give a physical description of him. In addition, a hotel that would attract sailors also would provide women for them. It concerned him that if he refused advances of a whore, it might appear he was gay, in which case the proprietor might send him a boy. Unhappy with the whole hotel idea, he would have to find some other place to get some sleep.

Deciding it was worth checking out how well guarded *Sea Urchin* was at night, he went to a bar to nurse a Cuban *Mojito* or two. He sat in a booth in a dark corner to avoid conversation, and waited until way past dark.

Around eleven, he paid his tab, shouldered his backpack and walked to the docks. Even though there were a couple of streetlights along the pier, they hardly gave much more than a gloomy glow, offering little light for seeing the guard's post under the gangway. Joe walked closer, heard snoring, and realized there was a soldier on duty, but very much asleep.

Taking out his flashlight, he put his fingers across the lens to re-duce the brightness and switched it on. Pointing it under the canvas canopy, he made out a man in uniform rocked back in the chair with his rifle beside him. His labored breathing indicated deep sleep. Joe switched off the light and looked around. There was no sign of anyone else close by. The ship was completely dark. *Was it too risky?* Maybe not. As quietly as he could, he went to the gangway, slipped under the 'no-trespassing' banner and eased up the aluminum stairs. As he stepped on the sixth step, it made a metallic creaking noise. Joe ducked down and froze, his heart pounding. Below there was a snort, a rustle and then a resumption of snoring. He took a couple of deep breaths. There were about a dozen more steps to the top. Having no choice now, he took another cautious step and then another. At the top, he looked back down and then scanned the roadway below, seeing no one.

From the top of the gangway, he stepped out onto the main deck near a crane that serviced a covered cargo hatch. In the gloom forward and above, he could make out the superstructure about one third of the length of the ship from its bow. He crossed over to the port side where he would not be seen from the pier. Climbing the stairs to the first level, he tried opening a steel watertight door but found it stuck, either with a lock inside or badly rusted. Another stair led up to the bridge. As he began to climb it, he heard the poom, poom, poom of an engine. A trawler was coming by in the bay. He ducked behind a vent pipe while the trawler passed by. It was rigged for fishing similarly to Seamus O'Leary's boat, and Joe shivered as he recalled his narrow escape from that thug during his mission in Northern Ireland.

He remained hidden until the craft had passed, its stern light re-flecting ripples in the dark bay below. He took one more look around and then made his way to the door of the bridge. Fortunately, that watertight door had been left open, leaving only an inner wooden door which was unlocked. He pushed it open, stepped over the raised threshold of the pilothouse, and closed it behind him. The ambient light from the dockside silhouetted the helm, an engine-order telegraph stand used to signal the engineer below, a few instruments, and a chart table.

Once again shielding the lens of his flashlight with his left hand, he switched it on with his right. It allowed only enough light for a quick inspection of the simple bridge equipment. Above the wheel were both a gyro compass repeater and an old magnetic and gimballed compass. He'd never get the gyro compass working, he guessed. In fact, it was questionable how much of the navigation gear—GPS—radio, radar, and so on he would ever make workable—not in a hurry anyway. Nothing in the pilot house would be of any use, he realized, without a reliable and skilled mechanic in the engine room. There would be no way to get the ship underway. He thought of Heinrich Heinz in a Cuban jail cell waiting to be interrogated and severely roughed up if not tortured. Of course, the guy would talk sooner or later. And then they would come after Joe. *What fool thing had he gotten himself into this time?*

He looked at the dark passageway aft of the pilothouse. He had been told the electronic spy gear was housed in that area hidden behind a false bulkhead. He shined the light on it and found the concealed door into the room. It occurred to him to look inside to be sure that the equipment was still there. It would make him feel mighty foolish to get the ship out of Havana only to learn that the spyware had been removed by the Cubans. That couldn't be the case however, he realized, because the world would have heard about it long ago.

Risking the full brightness of his flashlight, he scanned the bulkhead and found screw heads with the paint slightly abraded around them. He considered finding a screwdriver to remove them and see if the equipment indeed was there, but then he realized there were three reasons not to. One was that he might not be able to put the panel back in place, which would expose everything to any Cuban who might come up here. The second was the old principle of handling classified material—he had no "need to know." And the third was, whether the electronic equipment was back there or not, it was still his duty to confiscate the ship. He took one more look at the hidden door and thought about how he might well be studying the interior of a jail cell door of a Cuban prison. *No point in thinking about that.*

Joe found the interior stairway from the bridge and went down to the next level. It housed the sleeping spaces for the captain and other officers. Down the next level he found crew quarters, a large dining/living salon, and a galley, including a pantry. In the pantry he found the rancid odor of decaying foodstuffs. Fresh vegetables and fruit had not been thrown away. He opened the large refrigerator that had been without power for weeks and nearly fell over trying to close it in a hurry. Then behind him was a noise—a rustling. He jerked around, his heart pounding. Something scurried away. He saw that a fifty-gallon storage bin had its lid ajar. He peeked in and saw the disgusting morass of rat droppings and meal worms. Nearly gagging, he put the top back on securely. Yes, the ship had rats—lacking properly installed rat guards on the mooring lines. The thought of sharing quarters with them, however, caused him to shiver. He hated the vermin. Looking around further, he discovered shelves of canned goods, vegetables, soups, tuna, salmon, ham and several cases of bottled water. Fortunately, there was sufficient food for a trip to Florida and then some. All he had to do was get this baby out to sea and back to Miami. *Nothing to it. Ha!*

He went to the interior side of the door to the weather deck that he had tried unsuccessfully to open from outside. He unlatched it easily from the inside and started to push it open. Then he thought it unwise to leave it unlocked, for fear that some guard might find it and become suspicious. He shut it and dogged it down as he had found it and went back up to go out the pilot house door.

Once more in the pilot house, he decided to check out the charts. In his backpack, he had a harbor chart and a seaway chart, but he was heartened to find a better chart of Havana's main channel and approaches. The thought of running aground during the escape from the harbor with the Cuban coast guard bearing down on the ship would be an unimaginable disaster.

Making sure that everything was back in its proper place so that no one would notice he had been there, Joe eased open the door and stepped out on the deck of the bridge. He went down the same ladder on the seaward side and walked cautiously across the main deck to the gangway. Seeing no one along the quay, he stepped out on the first step and then froze. Rising from the guard's shelter below was a faint cloud, reflecting the dim yellow light. It was cigarette smoke, or cigar smoke most likely. The guard was awake and probably alert.

Joe stepped back on deck and tiptoed to a shadowy spot behind the crane. He put his hand to his head and blew out a big sigh. How long would the guard be awake? Until dawn? Joe could never get off the ship in daylight. Was he trapped aboard? *Oh God, now what?*

He made his way down the starboard side past the cargo hole to the stern. Two 20-foot long lifeboats hung from inverted hook-shaped Welin davits. The one pair to port was swung inboard, but the other was rigged outboard on the starboard side of the stern. The manila lines were coiled and secured to cleats at the rail, apparently with enough length so that one man could lower it while standing within the boat. He looked down and estimated the water line about twenty feet below. He uncoiled one of the lines and tripped the latch, taking a slight strain in his hands. He lowered the bow of the boat about a foot, causing only a slight creak in the line, no more noise than the ship's mooring lines made when the ship tugged on them in the wind. He pulled the boat back up to its original position and tied off the line.

That's one way to get off the ship, he decided, *if I'm lucky enough not to be seen*. He walked softly back to the gangway and peered over. Muffled voices from the guard station below indicated that two men were there. He stepped back from the side when one man appeared and then began walking off down the dock. It must be a change of the watch, Joe guessed. So far, the guards below had appeared lackadaisical and undisciplined enough to sleep on duty—a court-martial offense in the military he knew.

Deciding he'd have to give the new guard time to grow bored and begin napping, Joe thought he might as well take a look at the engine spaces. Since all doors seemed to be locked except for the one at the bridge, he climbed back up, entered, and put his backpack down in a corner.

He wound his way down the interior stairs to the main deck. There he found a horizontal hatch with four-inch combing above the deck. In the hatch was a vertical ladder to the first deck and then another hatch and ladder down to the engine spaces. Joe never did like being in the below-deck spaces of a ship, suffering mild claustrophobia. Even after shining the full beam of his flashlight down the stairs, he found the cramped and totally darkened bowels of an unknown vessel eerily creepy. The odor of oil and diesel fuel didn't help. He felt his way down to the bottom and stepped gingerly on a steel grid platform beside the main engine. By this time his flashlight had grown noticeably dimmer, making the tangle of wires and pipes feel like a great spider web. Shaking himself to ward off the panicky feelings, he spotted an emergency lantern hanging nearby. He switched it on and was happy to see that the batteries were good. He took it down and used it to inspect the equipment.

Attached to the drive shaft of the main diesel was the ship's main generator. Even though the insulation on the wiring looked worn, it looked okay overall. Nearby was an auxiliary generator powered by a small diesel engine, which had a manual hand crank starter for starting the big engine in an emergency. *Good!* Shining the light through the grid decking, he found the bilge pump below. Some water stood alongside the rusting keel. Considering it had not been pumped in some time, that amount of leakage appeared satisfactory. The hydraulic steering gear also looked okay. Without an engineer or two, however, no matter what shape everything was in, he simply could not navigate the ship. He could not manage the engine by himself, even if he could get everything started and running. Where the hell would he find an engineer?

Noting it was about a quarter past one, he yawned and felt tired enough to risk a few hours' sleep. As quietly as possible he crept back to the captain's quarters. The plumbing in the head, which depended on pumps didn't work, of course, but both the wash basin and the toilet had auxiliary hand pumps. Washed and relieved, he sat on the bunk and thought nothing could have felt better. Setting the alarm on his cell phone for four, he dared remove his boots, pistol and holster. Lying back on a soft pillow, he turned off his flashlight and soon fell fitfully asleep.

When his alarm went off, he bolted off the bunk, his pulse pounding. After calming down, he put his shoes on, used the toilet again and quietly peered out the porthole. It had been raining, and there were wisps of fog over the bay. As he started to sling the pack on his shoulder, it occurred to him that the thing was an annoying burden. Besides, carrying it around surely looked unusual and made him stand out.

Dumping the contents onto a table, he studied his sparse equipment. For weapons he had a commando's knife and a bottle of cyanide pills, meant for any opposition, and in the worst case, for himself. Military guards could be a real threat, of course, requiring him to take whatever defensive action was required. He scrutinized each item, weighing its value. There was no need for the harbor chart since there were better ones in the ship's pilot house. That was one item he could leave in a drawer. He looked at his Glock 19 pistol and ankle holster, considering what use a gun was to him anyway. Should he even carry the pistol? Suppose he was arrested and searched? How would he ever talk his way out of that? Reluctantly, he strapped the holster to his right ankle again and checked to ensure the gun was hidden under his pants leg.

He decided the extra clips of ammo were likely unnecessary. If he ever actually had to shoot someone, one or two bullets would be sufficient—maybe three because he likely would need one for himself if the situation deteriorated to a gunfight. *Enough of that thought!* He extracted a lightweight blue rain poncho. It would be handy at sea but not really required ashore. He recalled one summer visit to Charlotte Amalie, St. Thomas when people walked down the sidewalk oblivious to a downpour. When the rain stopped, everybody simply let the sunshine dry them off. Wouldn't it be nice to take Mary on a cruise to the Virgin Islands aboard *Tartan*. Maybe someday. He shook himself to get rid of the idea that this mission to Cuba was a foolhardy venture, and very likely a final one.

With a last look around, he spotted an unopened pack of Marlboros resting in a cubbyhole near the bunk. Seeing it brought back memories of his younger two-pack-a-day habit of many years. On a whim, he picked up the pack and put it in his pocket. He wouldn't dare smoke one, of course, knowing that the old addiction lay in wait, ready to strike him if he took even one puff. When the Cubans stand me before the firing squad, he ruminated, perhaps they will allow me to smoke one then.

As he picked up his burdensome backpack and opened the door to go out on deck, he realized that a stiff wind had arisen. Making his way down the ladder to the main deck, he crossed over to the gangway and peered down. There was no sign of a guard, but one surely was under the shelter. Seeing no one was in sight, he decided to chance going down the gangway. Thankfully, the wind gusts shoved the ship to a strain against its mooring lines and caused the aluminum gangway to creak, disguising his footsteps.

As he stepped onto the dock, he saw the silhouette of the guard, his rifle slung to his shoulder, peering out of his shelter but not looking his way. After an instant of panic, Joe made himself turn and walk straight toward the guard.

The man saw him, unslung his Kalashnikov rifle and pointed it at Joe with surprising swiftness.

"*Deténgase o disparo!*" the guard commanded and clicked off the safety. Joe froze, swallowed and tried to muster a pleasant tone of voice.

"*Hola,*" he called out. "*Qué agradable es esta hora temprana.* How pleasant it is this early hour."

The guard stared at Joe, still aiming his rifle, but seeming more surprised than anything. "*¿De dónde vienes?*" Despite the gloom, Joe recognized him as the old soldier, Hermano.

"*El barco de alii, señor Hermano.*" Joe replied pointing toward the red ship moored astern of *Sea Urchin*. "Just couldn't sleep."

"*No debes jugar con un hombre armado.* You shouldn't slip up on an armed man," he warned. "It's a good way to get shot."

Joe forced a big grin. "*Disculpas, amigo,*" he said as jovially as he could. "Didn't mean to surprise you. Just wanted some conversation." On impulse, he pulled out the pack of Marlboros, opened it, put a cigarette between his lips and offered one to the guard. "Here, *amigo.* Got a light?"

The man looked at the pack for a moment, gave a shrug and laid his rifle aside. He reached up and took one and fumbled in his pocket. Producing a lighter, he thumbed the flint and held the flame for Joe.

"*Gracias.*" The guard said and blew smoke.

"*De nada,*" Joe replied, inhaling for the first time in years. He coughed, and the fat soldier laughed.

"Strong cigarette. You must have had these for a while."

"Trying to quit," Joe lied, realizing the abandoned pack of Marlboros had been sitting around ever since the ship had been impounded. No wonder they were a bit stale.

Hermano tossed his cigarette in the water, reached in his breast pocket and pulled out two thin cigars. "*Aqui, chico, prueba uno de estos son frecos.*" He held one out to Joe.

Joe tossed his Marlboro and took the cigar. As he did so, a light rain began to fall, and the two of them stepped back under the makeshift canopy.

"*Dime tu nombre de nuevo, amigo,*" the guard asked as he held his lighter to Joe's cigar. Joe puffed to get it going.

"It's Joe," he replied.

"*¿De dónde eres?*"

"I'm from Toronto," he said recalling the city shown on his passport. It was very unlikely, he realized, that the guard would know anything about Canada, which was good because Joe knew little about Toronto himself. He sought to change the subject.

"Tough duty. *Es un deber duro.*" he remarked, "having to be out here at night."

The soldier shrugged. "*Toda una vida.*"

"Have you been in the military a long time, señor?"

"Ever since the Revolution," Hermano replied with a sigh. "*Desde entonces.*"

"Did you see Fidel Castro then. I mean, was he close to his fellow rebels?"

Hermano laughed. "Fidel and I were friends."

"You knew him personally?"

"We were boys in Biran, in Oriente Province—so filled with ideals and optimism. *Si, señor.* We were like brothers then..." He looked far away. "Such a glorious time for us and for Cuba."

"And after the victory, did you serve in the government? I mean, surely you enjoyed the winning, the spoils of war, or whatever?"

The old man shook his head. "I am a poor man, Joe. I had no education, no way to hold an office." He shrugged. "And then came the Russians. No. A man like me knows only how to fight and shoot a gun." He paused and puffed on his chico. "No. My wife and I struggled, in fact. And Sara became sick in childbirth and died when we were still young." Hermano shook his head and glanced at Joe.

"*La vida no es fácil, señor.* Life is not easy."

As rain pelted in a muted staccato on the canvas above them, the ancient soldier fell quiet. With sudden regret, Joe remembered that this man was his enemy. To carry out his mission of stealing the ship, he might have to shoot a guard, and a terrible sickening feeling came upon him as he realized it could be Hermano. He stood there in the veil of silence between them and felt that being a spy was being a traitor somehow, not to his country but to mankind in general. Joe let out a deep breath.

"*Te ha molestado la historia de mi vida?*" Hermano asked. "*No quise molestarte.* I did not mean to disturb you."

Joe gazed at the old man a moment and then offered his hand to shake.

"*Mi amigo,*" he said.

They smiled, and each took a drag on their cigars. Joe noticed that his own pants leg had ridden up enough to reveal the ankle holster. He glanced at Hermano and hoped the guard had not seen it. *Damn!* As casually as he could, he turned so that his right side was away from the guard. Apparently, the old man was relaxed and unwary.

They finished smoking, and Joe stamped out the butt. "Better be on my way," he said.

"*Hasta la vista,*" Hermano said pleasantly. Joe strongly hoped they would not see one another again.

With a wave, he picked up his backpack, stepped out in the rain and jogged toward the red ship, resisting the urge to turn around. When he reached the gangway of the Russian ship, he dared then to look back. Hermano was not to be seen, likely settling back in his chair, ready for another little *siesta*.

The rising sun was breaking through the clouds. Joe noticed it was not rainwater that dripped from his nose but nervous perspiration. Joe crossed the dock to the shadows of the warehouse building. He was about to walk away when an olive drab car, a Chevy of 1950's vintage with a failing muffler, putted up near *Sea Urchin* and stopped. A middle-aged soldier, in a uniform similar to Hermano's but neatly pressed, got out of the car, carrying an automatic rifle. He walked over to the dozing Hermano and kicked him in the leg.

"*Despierta, viejo!*" he shouted at the old soldier. Hermano stirred and slowly stood up and stretched.

"It's Revolution Day, in case you don't know it," the younger guard snapped.

"*Feliz Dia de la Revolución para ti, Carlos,*" Hermano replied sarcastically. "As if a young pup like you knew anything about the Revolution."

"*No hay mierda para ti, viejo,*" this Carlos replied. "And remember, you are to relieve me at six tonight. Don't be late. My wife and I have a party to attend."

"Oh, I would never want to inconvenience you, *camarada*," Hermano replied with disdain.

Carlos sneered as he tossed the car keys to Hermano. The old soldier failed to catch them, and they fell to the ground. He bent over to pick them up.

"*Adios, torpe*," the younger man said. Without comment, Hermano put his rifle in the old military car, climbed in and drove slowly away.

"Now, I could shoot that Carlos son of a bitch," Joe mumbled to himself. "That's no way to treat anybody, and certainly not that old man."

• CHAPTER EIGHT •

"The Big Breakfast," Joe said grumpily when Marsha came with a glass of water and pad to take his order. Only minutes ago, he had completed a phone call with Adams, who said, so far, they had found no new engineer.

"This ain't no frigging McDonald's, dearie," the waitress replied. "And where did you sleep? In a gutter already?" She eyed him disdainfully while Joe tried to smooth his cowlicked hair.

"I need some coffee, two cups, with cream." He rubbed his eyes and tried to smile at her.

"So, are you homeless or what?" Joe grimaced at her snide question. He really did not feel like talking.

"Just bring me some coffee, two eggs, uh three eggs maybe, toast, fruit, ham, whatever, please."

"Poor baby." She shook her head and went off to turn in his order.

He was still steaming about the lack of assistance from CIA. *You're a resourceful guy*, his handler Adams said, after relating the disappointing news that no engineer was being spirited his way. He kept stewing over this until Marsha sloshed a big mug of coffee on the table. Man, it smelled good.

"Back with your breakfast in a jiff." Someone at a far table called to her. "All right, all right. Keep your shirt on, Mac, I'm coming." She glanced at Joe. "No manners in this place, know what I mean?" She shook her head and bustled off.

Joe grinned and sipped the steaming coffee. The hot liquid went down his parched throat and immediately made him feel better. By the time his waitress friend came toward him with breakfast, he was ready for more coffee. She set in front of him a plate of fried eggs with ham. fried potatoes, some sliced pineapple and papaya.

"Cuban bread coming. I told Paco to fix you up." She stood there and watched as Joe scooped up a huge bite of potatoes. "Hungry, huh?" she said with a doting sort of smile. "I'll bring more coffee."

As he wolfed down the eggs, Joe looked at his backpack sitting in the booth beside him. Not only did he lack a great plan, he also had damn little equipment to use—not that there was anything short of a platoon of armed marines that could help.

On the face of it, there seemed to be only one guard at a time stationed at the bottom of the ship's gangway. For the next few hours it was that surly Carlos. But that guard station had a phone and an entire army and police force at his beck and call. Certainly, Joe had slipped aboard the ship undetected at night when Hermano slept. But wouldn't even Hermano become suspicious if Joe kept showing up? So how was he going to get a mechanic aboard and even a deck hand or two without a violent confrontation? With his head pounding from the lack of sleep, forging a plan at this point seemed nearly impossible. Although having a good meal was helping, his spirits needed more boost than that.

"Here's your toast," Marsha said as she put a large plateful down. "Don't eat the green leaves in the bread. They use palmetto to separate loaves. And here's butter and mango jam." He nodded his thanks and noticed she was giving him a lot of attention.

"I appreciate you explaining that to me," he said. She smiled.

Joe nodded and smiled back. It appeared he had found an ally in this unfortunately displaced woman.

"Say," she said. "The police are looking for a guy from the States. They apprehended some immigrants and some German character."

Joe did his best not to react. "Yeah? Where'd you hear that?"

"It's been on TV. They say to keep an eye out for an American and are offering a reward for any info." She looked quizzically at Joe. "Just thought you'd like to know."

"*Marsha, sirve estos platos!*" came the call from the kitchen.

"Okay, okay!" She gritted her teeth and rushed off.

Joe toyed with the bread and strange leaves, upset by the news. He pulled his phone out to see if he could have missed a call from Adams. What the hell was he going to do, he asked himself, and then became aware of someone approaching. It was Hosea.

"*Buenos dias, amigo,*" Hosea said as if greeting an ole buddy.

"Hell, we shouldn't be seen together. How'd you know I was here?"

Hosea slid into the booth across from him. "*Un hombre que le sigue el estómago,*" he replied, rubbing his stomach.

"Is that some cute Cuban expression?" Joe groused, looking to see if anyone was noticing them.

"No, actually, I made it up myself," Hosea laughed.

"Well, try this one out. "*Vamos. Vente antes de que venga la policia.*"

"But, Joe, we are partners in crime, remember?" He was interrupted by Marsha coming to take his order. She smacked down a coffee cup, filled it, and refilled Joe's. He waved at Joe's plate. "Bring me whatever he had, *por favor.*"

"Have you heard anything about Fernando?" Joe asked.

"Sadly, he is in jail. So is Heinz. The police are after both of us as well."

"So that asshole German did talk," Joe hit his fist on the table. Hosea shook his head and put his finger before his mouth in warning.

"I do have some good news for you, *compadre*. I have found an engineer for you. You do still need such a man, right?"

Joe sat up. "Damn right, I do! Who? I mean, is he qualified on big marine diesels?"

"Many years experience, I hear. At one time, he was one of the most knowledgeable in all of Cuba."

Marsha came and placed Hosea's plate on the table. "Did you see who came in a minute ago?" she whispered, nodding toward the front.

Joe saw two men in dark pants and shirts, each with a curious looking earpiece attached to a curly wire running to a vest pocket. If these were supposed to be undercover federal agents, they sure were easy to spot. He exchanged anxious glances with Hosea. Marsha looked from one to the other and seemed to realize their predicament. Already she had been suspicious of this attractive Joe character.

"I'll go distract them," she said and hurried away before Joe could deny his concern.

"You had better leave first," Hosea said. "Look, there's a bar a few blocks from here, called *El Escondite*. Meet me there at four this afternoon, and I'll introduce you to Felipe Lopez, *el mechánico.*" Hosea began making a sandwich out of his breakfast and wrapping it in a napkin. *"Ahora vete."*

"See you at four," Joe said. He stood, left more than enough pesos on the table, and looked for a path of escape. The two agents were questioning some merchantmen seated near the front door. Then he saw Marsha motioning toward the kitchen.

Joe walked casually in that direction, took his moment, and pushed through the door. A chef and a woman assistant bent over the stove hardly noticed him. He spied the outer door, went to it, exited and found himself in the alley.

"My backpack!" he all but shouted. "Damnation!" He had left it in the booth. Anyone who found it would be instantly richer. If the police got it, it would give them a way to trace him. Almost as quickly as he could kick himself again, Marsha opened the door and handed it to him.

"Forget something, sweetie?"

"Oh, God! Thank you!" he said, taking it from her. "You are a savior." He strapped it on. "I must be slipping."

"You're just tired, that's all. You look like a wet cat. Smell a little like one, too." She reached in her pocket and pulled out a key on a string. "Here's the key to my apartment. Go there and take a shower, will ya? And get some sleep."

Joe began to shake his head. "Oh, thanks but I couldn't impose..."

"Impose, smose," she cut him off. "Look, I really want you to." She pulled out her order pad and wrote down address. "And don't worry about Maria. She's out anyway, I think." She thrust the paper and the key in his hand. "Go. No arguments. *Nos pillamos*, as they say."

Joe studied her face a moment and realized she was a very lonely person who had become very attracted to him. There was something so sincere in her he knew she could be trusted. He disliked the thought of using her, but perhaps he could compensate her somehow, maybe give her enough CIA money to help her get back to New York or whatever. He wasn't sure exactly about how she was feeling about him, well, personally.

That *"nos pillamos"* statement seemed to carry some what? Sexual meaning? And he did not desire another tryst, or any sort of feminine relationship—especially not after the way Mary had reacted about his leaving.

But the idea of having a place to crash was greatly appealing. He gave Marsha his best smile.

"You're a real friend," he said.

• • •

"MARY," FRANCES SAID LOUD enough to be heard over the din of conversation on the Havana tour bus. "You're not paying attention."

"I'm sorry, what were you saying?" Mary realized that she had tuned Frances out at the moment. It was difficult to remain focused on everything Frances said because her companion kept up an uninterrupted stream of comment.

"Say, how old is this humpback bus? Fifty, sixty years? Smells like it, don't you think? Glad we have the windows open. I love the street sounds anyway, don't you? I hope we stop soon. I really need a coffee and… You suppose they grow coffee here? I love native things, especially when they come from the very place where you are. But then I guess that's what makes them native and all…"

The bus driver turned right into a parking lot beside a cemetery.

"Here we see *El Cementerio de Cristóbal Colón*," the guide droned, "also called *La Necrópolis de Cristóbal Colón*. The first people to be buried there were…"

"*Colón*," Frances repeated loudly. "They buried colons here? Wouldn't you think they would have interred the entire body, for goodness sakes." From the few snickers and groans, Mary could tell they all had come to expect something out of the ordinary from Frances. She turned to Mary.

"You're not listening again. Oh, I'll bet you're thinking about Joe, aren't you? Listen, girl, men do lots of silly things. They haven't got any sense. Look at Alex. He's off in New York probably trying to do some more insider trading, don't you imagine? Never learns. Oh well, *c'est la vie*. That's French, you know. I wonder how you say that in Spanish. Oh, Miss! Miss, uh, Whoever-o, como speako, um, *that's life* in Cuban? You know these cute people have got some funny expression for it, what do you think?

"Good question," she said to Frances. "I'm afraid I don't know anything other than just a literal translation. Èsta *es la vida,* or something." She turned to glance at the driver, noticed he was getting up and motioned to him.

Juan, as he had been introduced when the tour started, came back to them. He looked to be in his forties.

"*Que bola?*" he said. Mary was busily thumbing through her Berlitz in an effort to find the expressions.

"I want to say 'that's life' the way Cubans say it," Frances demanded. The driver smiled. He too had formed an opinion about Frances.

"*Asi est la vida,*" he said.

"Assy est la veed-ha," Frances repeated. "Did I say that right?"

His smile broadened. "We have another expression more common in Cuba. It's '*No es fácil.*' More or less the same thing."

"*Fácil* sounds like French for *easy,*" Frances replied. "Not easy? What's not easy?"

"*La vida,*" he said. "Nothing is easy. Life is not easy."

"Oh, come on now," Frances said. "Nobody ever said life was easy, but it seems to me you Cubans complain a lot. Probably learned that from the Communists. I bet you don't like being a Communist. Never mind: you don't have to answer that. Most everybody seems to think I go on too much, but I think if you have a thought, you ought to say it. Know what I mean?"

Mary nodded but continued staring out of the window, more conscious of her thoughts about Joe. Where on earth was he? Had he been captured in Kazakhstan? Was he under arrest in Russia or locked in some prison in Patagonia?

She was so worried. What a fool thing to do—going off to do some stupid thing for the CIA. *Maybe God takes care of fools and spies,* she hoped.

CHAPTER NINE

On the way to Marsha's apartment for that much needed shower bath and nap, Joe continued to worry about finding an engineer. Even though Hosea had assured him his prospect was well qualified, Joe hoped to find a second choice, just in case. He stopped a man wearing a captain's cap and asked if he knew of any place where transient merchant sailors might be listed for employment.

"None that I know of, mate," said the captain with a ruddy face and Australian accent. "But I did spy a marine store up the street aways. Looks to be run by some bloody Russkies. I never like making port in Havana."

"I'm not so happy to be here either," Joe said.

Setting out in that direction, he noted the number of people on the streets had increased dramatically since nine o'clock, along with a surprising number of street vendors, likely because this was the big national holiday. A short plump man carried about five straw hats on his head, one stacked into the other, and a sixth in his hand, waving it at the passersby. Although the hat seller was not the least bit Hispanic in appearance, it did not prevent him from blending in the mélange of skin colors. Black, brown, swarthy, and light people swarmed around him on the sidewalks. A woman with skin as dark as leather led two very blond five-year-olds by the hand. The din of boisterous Cuban Spanish echoed off the cracked stucco walls of apartment buildings. Every balcony sported a national flag, some emblazoned with images of Fidel Castro and Che Guevara.

A beautiful brown-skinned girl with a revealing puffy white blouse was approaching him on the sidewalk. Joe gave her a casual onceover as he neared and was surprised that she very openly smiled and winked at him. He had heard that Cubans were a hot-blooded culture, to say the least. Suppressing the urge to look back, he kept on walking. This was no time for him to become involved with a *chica bonita*.

Up ahead was a sign overhanging the sidewalk with the word, *Diesel*, in big letters. Below the word was the name, *Kolomensky Zavod*. As he reread the sign, the name did not look Spanish; in fact, he realized it was undoubtedly Russian. Of course, he knew, even though Putin seemed to have little interest in Cuba these days, there surely were holdovers from the past. In fact, the store likely could still be run by Russians. Fighting off feelings of desperation, he thought even a Russian mechanic would be acceptable.

He was surprised to discover that the interior of the store looked much like a marine store combined with an auto parts shop. Rolls of thin yellow neoprene sat beside coils of 2" hemp mooring lines. Chrome shackles and cleats hung on display racks alongside shelves of oils and lacquers and waxes and solvents. Red CO_2 fire extinguishers of American make stood in a row on the floor, and five-gallon buckets of paint and boot topping and undercoat were stacked shoulder high. The place reeked a dank smell of oil and rats. Acting as if he were just browsing, Joe picked out a spray can of WD40 to carry with him to the counter.

Two men, one clearly Hispanic and the other swarthy Slavic with mixed blonde and brown hair, were busy at computer terminals of a brand he had not seen before.

Joe stepped up close to the man with the dirty blond hair and set the spray can on the counter. The clerk looked up at him with a bothered expression and kept on typing. After a minute or so, Joe realized this guy was not especially motivated to help him. Becoming irritated but knowing he needed to keep his cool, Joe took in a deep breath before speaking.

"Excuse me. Do you speak English?' He received another irritated look along with a shrug.

"Yah. What you want?" the man finally replied. He finished what he was keying into the computer and then stared icily at Joe.

"I, uh," Joe hesitated. The sign out front had named a Russian, and from his accent, the Slavic man must be Russian. The man looked Joe up and down and scowled.

"I wanted to buy this." He pushed the can closer.

"So? Where's your money?"

"Oh, of course," Joe said and pulled out his wallet. He started to hand over some Cuban pesos but thought better of it and instead pulled out some Cuban script called *cucs*, supplied for tourists to use. With the same surly expression on his face the man grabbed up the bill and began making change. Joe didn't like asking a Russian, of all people, but he decided to plunge in anyway.

"I'm looking for an engineman," he said. "A mechanic. Somebody who knows ship's diesels. Main engines, you know."

"To do what?" The unfriendly stare continued.

"I'm, uh, we are shorthanded in the engine room. I need someone who can join our crew."

"What ship?"

Joe grimaced. This guy was full of more questions than answers, and this question about what ship was a doozie. He thought fast.

"The ship's not arrived yet. It has Caterpillar diesels, are you familiar with the German Caterpillar, 3512D," he recited recalling the briefing with Hans at CIA. "Are you familiar with that model?" He was trying to turn himself into the asker instead of the answerer.

"Ha, 3512C-HD, you mean" the man corrected, clearly proud of his knowledge.

"You really know your stuff," Joe said, pretending admiration. "I see you have real experience."

"Forty-one years," the Russkie replied. "So when is the ship due in?"

"I'm not sure," Joe said. "It may be delayed by weather." The Cuban clerk, wiping his hands on his yellowed white shirt, wandered over, curious about their conversation.

"And how did you get here?" The Russian's eyes narrowed with a hint of suspicion. Joe had been warned that spies for the Cuban government would be crawling out of every rat hole, and a Russian was a likely candidate.

"I'm just a logistics rep for the shipping company," Joe said. "My job is to precede our ships into port, set up dockage arrangements, find people to make repairs in order to keep the turnaround sailing time short. You know what I mean?"

"I know of no mechanics," the man said, shaking his head. "Not any who want to sign on to a crew."

"We can put up a notice," the Cuban interrupted, his demeanor much more hospitable. "Another place to ask is at the café down the street." Joe smiled at him.

"How can we contact you if someone turns up?" the Russian asked. Joe managed to smile at him, too.

"I'm not checked into a hotel yet," he said. "I'll let you know as soon as I've settled in somewhere. Maybe by then I'll know when our ship's due."

"Your ship's arrival likely will be delayed, señor," the Cuban replied. "We have a tropical storm coming."

"A storm? Man, that's all we need, isn't it?" he replied, honestly expressing concern. He picked up his change, the can of WD40. As he turned to leave, he felt the suspicious, steely cold stares behind him.

Isn't that great! Joe told himself as he left the store. Of course, there was no ship coming to help, storm or not. There would be no rescue, no sending in the cavalry or landing the marines. He looked up and down the street as if to see something to assist. Shaking his head, he started off for Marsha's apartment, thinking that at least he had one friend to help him through this nightmare. That shower bath was sure going to feel good.

• CHAPTER TEN •

"This doesn't look very communistic to me!" Frances exclaimed when they entered *El LIMONERO* for lunch and saw tables set with crystal glasses and white tablecloths. "I expected Russian-red décor myself."

"It looks a bit more elegant than I expected," Mary admitted. "I didn't think our tour fees would cover such as this." The maître d', who was seating all the tour patrons, approached, bowed slightly and motioned them to follow.

"Oh, I think we're entitled to being treated grandly," Frances replied, "we free Americans being bold explorers in a dictatorship country." They followed the man in black tie as he led them to their table and pulled out the chair for Frances. She sat primly and allowed herself to be pushed to the table. Mary sat herself and eagerly picked up the menu at her place.

"I wonder who will be seated with us," Mary said, indicating the two other places at the table.

"Oh, I hope it's not those two women from New Jersey," Frances sniffed, "Gladys and Mable, ohh. I cannot abide their accents and inane chatter." Mary lowered her face to hide her grin from her companion--*la cabra*, was the word?

"They may think our accents a bit unusual, don't you imagine?" she suggested.

"Now, Mary, you know we Southern ladies are by far the most genteel," Frances said. "The Yankees may have won the war, destroyed our economy and way of life, but they could not, cannot take away our refinement, dear. You know that. I'm just so thankful I grew up in Alabama, born to the descendants of planters, educated and refined people of the old South. No, dear, don't allow these modern-day women to destroy your heritage. We shall forever be…"

She was interrupted by the maître d's arrival with an older couple. With surprise, they realized the man was the one with the Cuban accent who had spoken up on the bus at the Revolution Museum.

"*Discúlpenme, señoras,*" The maître d' said. "We are very crowded today. I must seat these gentle people with you." As he spoke, he held the chair for the rather dumpy but well-dressed wife so that there could be no refusal. The woman's smile turned to grimace as the head waiter pushed her chair up.

"Sorry to barge in on you," she apologized then glanced at her husband who appeared to be hanging back.

"Alvaro," she said, beckoning to him, "please."

The man, with a slightly swarthy complexion and a neatly trimmed moustache that matched his dark massive eyebrows and dark hair, visibly sighed, nodded politely and sat across from Frances. Burying his face in the menu, he avoided eye contact.

"This has been a wonderful tour," Mary offered. "I hope you all are enjoying it as much as I am."

"Oh, yes, wonderful," the wife replied. She sat forward. "I'm Betty, and this is Alvaro." Her husband looked up to nod, his smile interrupting a sad expression, then quickly looked down again as if further studying the menu.

"We're from Dayton," Betty said. "I think you two must be from the South."

"We're from Birmingham," Mary answered. "Not quite so far from home as you," she quipped.

"You must be Cuban," Frances announced to the man, allowing no such avoidance of conversation. He glanced at her with a dignified nod, a restrained response as if caught in some misdeed.

"For Alvaro, this trip is a return home," Betty said.

"I enjoyed hearing you correct the tour guide this morning," Mary said.

"Yes," Frances added. "It was wonderful hearing someone disagree with all that commie propaganda she's been spouting."

"Alvaro himself was one of those students that took over Batista's palace."

"Betty, please," he interrupted and shot her a look.

"Are you not proud of that?" Frances surged on.

"It is very complicated," he said.

"Life is always complicated," Frances said. "We go from one emergency to another. If an emergency doesn't come up on its own, I usually try to stir one up." The comment got her a laugh, even from Alvaro, who relaxed a bit.

"So tell us about growing up in Cuba," Mary urged. "Tell us something about it that these tour people don't know. I'd like to hear." He looked away. "Maybe I'm being too forward," Mary apologized.

"Life's too short not to be forward," Frances said. "Keeping things back is a waste of time if you ask me. Why, I have to tell everything about myself, haven't you noticed? I even talk about how Alex goes up to New York to get all the insider dope from the stock market. That's why we can afford big boats and trips to Cuba and all such manner of things. So come on, Alvaro. I smell a story here. Let's have it, for goodness sake!"

The waiter came at that moment and interrupted Frances. She gestured impatiently and glanced at her menu.

"What is this 'Arrows con Polo'? Sounds like some kind of sporting event to me. Is this a Cuban dish, or a Commie one?" The waiter stiffened.

"*Arroz con Pollo,*" he sniffed. Only the grandest fare is to be served here." He raised an eyebrow at Frances. "I would hope you have the pallet to appreciate our haute cuisine."

"My, my," she replied. "They must have sent you to Paris or somewhere to learn how to insult your customers. Or maybe they sent you to Moscow for training in communist behavior."

Mary touched France's arm. "Perhaps we should just order, don't you think?" She gave an apologetic look to Betty, who seemed more amused than shocked. Mary and Frances stared at the menu a long moment.

"I have a wonderful idea," Betty said. "Let's ask Alvaro to order for all of us. I think we could not do better."

Even Frances thought that was a fabulous idea. Betty gave him a pleading look of encouragement. He shrugged, nodded and studied the menu, and selected for them.

"*Ropa vieja y ensalado de aguacate, Borro. … Poro y Piña.*"

The waiter bowed slightly to Alvaro, glanced a smirk at Frances, and rushed away.

"We'll be having pulled flank steak served over rice," Alvaro explained. "*Ropa vieja* means 'old clothes' because it looks like a pile of colorful rags. And we'll begin with a salad of avocado, watercress, and pineapple."

"Yum!" said Mary. "Wonderful."

"Well, now, where were we," Frances asked, "before that rude Soviet something or other disturbed us? Oh yes, Alvaro was going to tell us his life story, weren't you, Alvaro?"

"Why not, my darling?" Betty said. "I think it would help." She turned to Mary. "It took quite a bit of convincing to get Alvaro to come on this tour to Havana. Leaving his boyhood home at the time of the

Revolution was such a loss, a tragedy to him. I told him, however, that coming back would give him some closure, join the ends of a ring of anger and unhappiness that has plagued his life." She put her hand on his. "These are very nice ladies, dear, and I think it would do you good to tell your story."

"Oh, yes!" Frances exclaimed. "You could tell us, kind of like going to confession if you're a Catholic—I'll bet you're a Catholic, being Cuban and all. Or maybe it's like lying on a psychiatrist's couch and spilling the beans—I've done that many times, though, and I can't say it's done much for me, can you? But anyway, let's hear it. I'm so eager!" She leaned forward and stared at him expectantly.

He met her stare, glanced at Mary and at Betty, then at Frances again and chuckled.

"*Qué diablos. Por qué no?*" He took a deep breath. "If you wish, I will tell you. You see, my father owned and operated a sugar plantation. It was ten thousand acres, in my family for generations. We exported sugar to the United States and many other countries. I grew up learning the business from my father, who was a good manager and so kind and generous to his five hundred employees." His expression darkened.

"I was attending the university here in Havana in the 50's. Like most young people, I was an idealist and rebellious. In opposition to President Batista's dictatorship, my friends and I formed a political group in 1954, which we called *Directorio Revolucionario Estudiantil*. All of this was most disapproved of by my father, you understand. Three years later when our movement had grown, we stormed the Presidential Palace and took it for a time." He shook his head. "Then the communist insurgents under Castro overwhelmed our movement and threatened us. Fidel Castro and his band of *renegados, rebeldes*— freedom fighters, he called them. Ha! Freedom fighters backed by Soviet Communists—a contradiction in terms—a lie that took hold of the people and made them turn away from the good leaders like my father." He grew hoarse, emotional in the telling.

"And you fled to Miami, didn't you, dear?" Betty added. "In order to carry on your opposition to Castro?"

"Castro's army took over our plantation, our home, dragged him away…" Alvaro had tears coming, eyes red with anger. "They murdered my father, you see. And I was not there to help him, to defend…" His voice broke and his shoulders heaved in sobs. Betty leaned over and hugged him tightly.

"It's all right," she whispered to him. "You should cry, my poor darling." She looked across the table at Frances. "It was so hard on him, you see. He was only twenty at the time."

"So sorry," Alvaro said, and squeezed his wife's hand. He pulled away gently, sat up, and wiped his eyes with his red cloth napkin. "Forgive me, ladies. I seldom show emotion."

"I am so happy you told us," Frances said with gentle sweetness. "I imagine that you needed to tell that. It is an important part of your trip back here to Cuba."

"I hoped this would be a catharsis for him," Betty said as she sat back and took his hand. "Perhaps now you can enjoy the rest of the tour with less anger and regret, Alvaro. Oh, I'm hoping so."

He wiped his eyes again. "Perhaps," he said, "but I doubt it." He attempted an apologetic smile at Mary. She returned it with a kind look.

"Did you participate in the Bay of Pigs invasion?" Frances asked.

Alvaro shook his head. "Not in that fiasco, no. Those of us DRE members in Florida did assist the CIA in intelligence gathering and communicating with other anti-communists in Cuba, but no."

"Oh, we know all about the CIA, don't we Mary? Right now, her boyfriend Joe Anderson is in some god-awful country somewhere doing some crazy thing for the…"

"Hush, Frances, please!" Mary interrupted. "We can't talk about that."

"Oh, pooh. Why not? We're here among friends." She spied the waiter coming toward them with a big tray. "Oh, goody!" She exclaimed. "Here comes lunch!"

• CHAPTER ELEVEN •

Looking for Marsha's apartment in the early afternoon, he walked to the main thoroughfare and turned left, beginning to break a sweat in the July heat. Unhappily, there was no shady side of the street, and the backpack made walking no easier. He bent down to re-adjust the ankle holster under his pants leg and walked on. Mary came to mind again. What would she say if she knew he was bound for a single woman's apartment? He also wondered if Marsha's generosity was in any way driven by sexual attraction. Although she was approachable enough, he felt no such feelings for her. Funny how some women held a certain magnetism while others did not. As grateful as he was for the use of her apartment, he was glad to be going there alone.

He passed a liquor store, noticed that it was open, and decided that it would be nice to buy Marsha a bottle of something. And besides, he needed a drink. Inside the tiny store he found unpainted wooden shelves bending under the weight of various brands of rum, a lot of vodka, and a little gin. A middle-aged black woman stood behind a counter, leaning over a magazine. She looked at him quizzically as if she thought his presence unusual. Self-conscious over his wrinkled clothes, Joe quickly selected a quart of Ron Rico and another of Bacardi Light and took them to the counter.

"*Es un buen dia,*" he said with a smile. The woman nodded, eyes down, and bagged the bottles.

"*Cuarenta y tres pesos.*"

Joe thought 53 pesos was too much to pay, but decided she

overcharged all *gringos*, and handed her the money. Without comment, she handed him his change and stared at his backpack as he picked up the sack and turned to go out. In his CIA briefing he had learned that many ordinary Cuban citizens became police informers as a way to make a little extra money from the government. Nervously, he hurried down the street, believing he had encountered just such a person. Had the police obtained his picture and aired it on television? He was getting more and more antsy. He came to the intersection with the busy *Carretera Casablanca* and waited for the light to change. Among the numerous passing vehicles, a double decker bus caught his eye. It had the name of some tour company on the side. As it went by, he noticed a blond woman staring out of the window at him.

• • •

"MARY, YOU LOOK AS if you had just stuck your hand in a light socket," Frances said. "Whatever is the matter?" Mary put her hand to her bosom and gasped a couple of deep breaths. As the bus moved on, she looked back but could no longer see the man in the crowd. Frances took her hand.

"What is it, dear?"

"I saw Joe," she said. "At least, I saw a man who... No, I really think I saw him."

"Where?"

"On the sidewalk, just back there…near the corner," Her voice jumped to falsetto. "He was just standing there, looking at me"

"Really?" Frances exclaimed. "I'll tell the driver to stop." She jumped up out of her seat. "HEY, JUANDO. STOP THE BUS!"

Everyone turned to look at Frances. The driver, Juan, slammed on the brakes. Mary grabbed her arm. "Wait, Frances. No," Mary whispered. "We can't say anything even if it was Joe. He's undercover. Please."

The driver was glaring at Frances in his mirror. An exasperated Señorita Madelena came down the aisle.

"Is something wrong?"

"Boy howdy, is something wrong! I'll tell you what. Poor Mary here has this boyfriend that's always going off and working for the CIA on crazy kinds of deals. He's a spy and all that. He's back there on the street—she just saw him—probably trying to pick up some young innocent Cuban girl or something, and sneaking around looking at secret stuff and, all the while, Mary, Oh, Poor Mary is just suffering the all-overs about him, and you'd think he would be more considerate and just go home and help her tend her garden—she has a lovely garden at her cute little bungalow home back in Birmingham—and this guy ought to have sense enough to realize what a fine arrangement he has with her. I'm hoping they'll get married someday and quit living, well, the way they are not being married, you know, but anyway, she needs to go back and tell him to act right and go home and..."

"Frances, please!" Mary said. "Hush."

"Well, goodness knows you love him," Frances said. "So I'll be quiet about it—hush, hush, as you say. But really..." Frances finally ran out of breath. Everyone was staring in rapt attention, and then a pudgy man in his sixties that was sitting nearby let out a 'yuk' and everybody on the bus burst into laughter.

"It's all right," Mary plead to the tour guide. "Let's just move on." Behind the bus several car horns were blaring.

"*Una cabra,*" Juan mumbled as he started the bus again. "*esta como un cabra.*"

The two ladies sat silently while the guide continued her droning about the sights along the street. Mary pretended to be interested, but she could not get Joe off her mind. *What is he doing here? Is he in any danger? How long will he stay?* What is it that motivates a man like Joe to do these wild things? she wondered. As if in love with a stunt pilot, a Navy Seal, or a race car driver, she worried about his safety, his very survival, and somehow that worry only heightened her feelings for him. If only there was some way to share adventures with him again, facing the dangers as they had done together during their perilous passage aboard Frances' and Alex' sailboat, *Mission*. If only it were possible to go to him, to find him, to be with him some way.

"So what are we going to do?" Frances said, breaking Mary's train of thought.

"We can't do anything, Frances," Mary replied. "We have to finish our tour and not concern ourselves with it."

"I've got it!" Frances nearly shouted, her expression brightening. "When we get back to the hotel, we can change into our outfits—the Cuban dresses we bought—and then take a cab back down here. Oh, yes! We can put on lots of makeup and become, what's the word? Undercover...INCOGNITO. We'll come down here and find Joe—if it is Joe—and spy on him."

"Frances, what are you saying? Ridiculous. We can't do anything to..."

"Oh, delicious!" Frances whispered even louder. "Just think. We'll be spies, agents, James Bond and Nancy Drew all balled into one. Imagine, Mary. Oh terriffs! I'm so glad I thought of this, aren't you?" She beat her feet up and down on the floor of the bus. "I can hardly wait!"

Mary stared at Frances, drew in a deep breath between her gritted teeth, and then laughed out loud. *Of course! Why not?*

• • •

THERE WERE SEVERAL people standing around talking on the sidewalk near the front door of Marsha's apartment building. A woman with markedly Hispanic features but with black skin was engaged in some banter with a man much younger. Children under five climbed on the iron bannisters. They all stopped and stared as Joe approached. He smiled, said *"Buenos Dias,"* and went up the steps and inside as quickly as he could. In the dark hallway he bounded up the stairs and found the door to number 11. The key turned easily, and Joe went in and closed the door. He looked around, fully expecting an animal to come out to greet him.

"Here Maria, here," he called. That was the name of the pet, Maria? Nothing appeared, so he knew it wasn't a dog. A cat wouldn't come and might even hide. He shrugged. Maybe it's a bird or something, an iguana or whatever. Just so long as it wasn't a snake.

The small living room was dominated by a worn leather sofa and two cane chairs situated around a low coffee table made of two kegs and a mahogany-stained board across them. On an end table beside the sofa stood a lamp fashioned after the Statue of Liberty and topped with a faded green lamp shade. He guessed this lamp was a reminder of home.

A tiny kitchen had a sink full of dirty dishes, and a pot of some dried-up *frijoles* sat on the two-burner stove. There was a small ice tray in the little fridge, and he decided to fix a glass of ice water. On impulse he opened the Bacardi and poured himself a stiff drink, which he drank and then poured another. The buzz came on quickly.

He went to the bedroom door and peered in, seeing twin beds covered with wrinkled blue sheets pulled over to cover bumpy mattresses. Joe went in the small adjoining bathroom, lifted the seat on the toilet and relieved himself. Still no pet to be seen. In the full-length mirror on the door, he saw just how wrinkled and salty his clothes were. Fatigued as he was, he decided he had to shower. He kicked off his shoes in the bedroom, unfastened the holster from his ankle, and hid it under the bed. Going into the small bathroom and turning on the shower, he discovered there was no hot water tap, but the shower stream was warm enough just from the summer heat. He got in, clothes and all.

It felt great. He stripped off the sodden clothing and washed himself. Then he turned off the water, grabbed a towel off the rack and dried. Gathering up his clothes, he wrung them out and hung them up.

Realizing it would take a while for his clothes to dry, he wrapped the towel around him and sat on the bed. He drained the glass of rum, noticed he was slightly dizzy, and resisted having any more. Attracted by sight of the bed, as unkempt as it was, he found it very inviting if not compelling. Deciding that Marsha would not be coming home anytime soon, he laid down on top of the blue sheet, closed his eyes and fell deeply, soundly, uncaringly asleep.

• • •

HE FELT THE MATTRESS SINK as if Mary were climbing in bed or turning over or something—a usual and comfortable thing. His eyes still closed, he became conscious of a hand stroking him gently, giving him an erection. Oh good… but something was wrong. In the dim fog of sleep, he began to remember he was not in Birmingham, but in Cuba, and in his wooziness, he was aware of lying naked in a strange bed and someone was touching him. A leg was across his groin. He opened his eyes and looked over. A tawny buxom nude lay beside him, smiling. In a smooth, almost acrobatic move, she was on top and inserting his erection.

"*Hola sexy alli*," she said. "*Hombre guapo.*" For a moment he succumbed to the pleasure, but then he came to enough to sense a violation of will in the suddenness of the situation. Then he was about to come, and it fully awakened him. Shocked by the situation, Joe flung himself off the bed and fell to the floor, bumping his head on the bedside table. He sat up and looked at her. She turned on her side to face him and laughed.

"Who are you?" he stammered. "Uh, *Qui*, uh, *quién eres?*"

"*Me llamo Maria*," she replied with a Cheshire-cat grin, as she pulled herself over where she could peer over to see all of him better. "*Eres Joe, si?* Marsha told me you would be here," she went on in English, "but she did not say you would be so *desnuda y sexy.*" She reached over to touch him. "Why not come back up here, you pretty boy. *Tenemos una oportunidad para la diversión.*" She glanced at his now very limp condition.

"Oh, did you hurt yourself falling?"

Joe scrambled to his feet and turned sideways to her. "I need to go, uh, *necesito ir al baño.*" He hurried to the bathroom and shut the door. Truly he did need to go, but he also needed a chance to think this through. So this was the 'Maria' Marsha had told him not to worry about. A roommate-*compañera de cuarto. She won't bite, huh?*

While he used the toilet, he thought over his options. Obviously, the choice of a Cuban styled *fuki-fuki* loomed large. She surely knew how. But there was no way he was going to be unfaithful to Mary—not again.

Thankful he had not climaxed, there was no way he could consider such a thing, even with this rather attractive and desirable and extremely forward Maria. But how could he keep from making her angry? She certainly had thrown herself at him, and he knew the dangers of a wrathful woman. She might go to the police just out of spite. What a catastrophe that would be. And he surely couldn't kill her.

"Joey, Joey, *mi amante,*" she called from the other side of the door. "Come see if you like my *bollo.* It's asking for you." He stared at the door in confusion. Then he had an idea. A wonderful idea. He felt his underwear that had been drying on the towel rack. He put on the briefs, grabbed up his other clothes and opened the door. Maria was lying voluptuously on the bed.

"¿*Qué pasa?*" she asked with a frown. "*Quitate la ropa cariño.* Darling." Joe sighed and shook his head.

"I am so sorry, Maria," he said, putting on an act. "But I just never have been able to... Oh, it is so hard to say this... I am... well, gay."

"Ganso? Usted? No lo creo! I don't believe it."

Joe hung his head and sighed deeply. "Yes, it's true. All my life. I'm so sorry."

Maria puffed out her cheeks. *"La mierda,"* she said and yanked the sheet around her. She stood up and gave him a look of disgust.

"Lo siento mucho," he said with abject apology. She huffed as she brushed by going into the bathroom and slamming the door.

Joe breathed a great sigh of relief. His heart was pounding from a combination of shock and sexual frustration, and his head felt as big as a pumpkin. He grabbed up his damp clothes and put them on quickly. *Oh, what a hangover!* Strapping the pistol holster on his ankle, he managed to put on his shoes and take a deep breath before she opened the door. Maria thankfully had put on a robe.

Joe went into the living room, sat on a chair with a cover of big printed red camellias, and wondered what the hell to do next. There was the sound of a key in the lock. The door opened, and Marsha greeted him.

"Hope you got some rest," she said. "Oh, I see your clothes are a bit wet."

"Your roommate is here."

"Oh? Did Maria come home? I hope she didn't disturb you or anything."

Joe grimaced. "Uh, oh no," he said. "We got along okay." Maria marched into the living room still buttoning her blouse.

"Si, we got along," she said with emphatic sarcasm. "Your *gringo* is a very sweet boy."

Marsha looked piercingly at her roommate. "What, Maria? What do you mean by that?"

Joe spoke up, putting on his sad and apologetic face again. "I hope I haven't inconvenienced you all by being here. I really appreciated the opportunity to take a nap." He started toward the bedroom. "Let me gather up my stuff, and I'll be on my way."

While he closed his backpack, he heard the women discussing him in hushed tones. He heard Maria say "*Pájaro*," which he did not recognize but guessed it was not a compliment. He checked the time. It was about 5:30. When he went back in the living room, he could tell from Marsha's expression that Maria had told her about his "condition."

"Thanks again," Joe said as he headed for the door. "I'll be on my way now."

"Wait," Marsha said. "Where are you going?"

"I have to go meet someone at a bar, uh... *El Escondito.* Can you tell me where it is?

"I'll go with you," Marsha said.

Joe hesitated. "Okay, but can we get there by six?"

"Only if we walk. The traffic out there's terrible. It's not too far."

He went to the door and turned to look at Maria. "*Perdoname*," was all he could think to say. He really was not very happy with them believing he was queer, but it seemed best to leave it at that.

• CHAPTER TWELVE •

"**B**ut don't you guess he'll recognize us?" Mary asked. She was adjusting the ruffled red and yellow skirt to her shapely waist. Although she and Frances were putting on the garish outfits they had bought in the boutique dress shop, Mary still had reservations about her friend's scheme for the evening.

"After I finish making up our faces," Frances replied, "even you won't recognize us." She had opened the pancake makeup from the costume store and was applying it thickly to her own face. All we need is to give ourselves a swarthy complexion and a bit of rouge and lipstick the way these Cuban women do it."

If Mary harbored any misgivings about going to find Joe, she felt driven by a mixture of both concern and curiosity. As long as he didn't realize they were there, then how could it matter that she and Frances would be spying on him a little. She glanced at the hotel room window and noted the sun was beginning to set. After returning to the hotel, everyone had gone to their rooms for a brief rest and change of clothes before cocktail hour and dinner at a nearby restaurant.

"I'm sorry we are going to miss supper," Frances said. "I was counting on a drink and a good meal."

"This is their biggest holiday, so I'll bet it was going to be something special," Mary agreed. "But if that really was Joe we saw..."

"We must press on, absolutely!" Frances said. "Mischief first, food second, I always say."

"Don't worry. Where we're going, I'll bet we can find some real authentic Cuban cuisine—not just tourist fare. And we'll make Joe pay for it." Frances stared in the mirror, cocked her head and frowned at the cleavage showing above the neckline of her ruffled purple blouse. With a sigh, she applied even more tan powder to her neckline.

"It's not easy," Frances said. "Isn't that what these people are always saying about life?" She shook her head at herself and turned to gaze at Mary. "I'll tell you what; the first time Alex saw me, he was knocked out. But at this age, well, anyway… Come over here, Mary girl, you younger-than-I little thing, unfairly so, dammit, and let me help with your makeup." She stood up and motioned demandingly with the powder puff.

Reluctantly, Mary went over and sat at the dressing table. "Just a little will do, I think."

"Hush and hold your hair up out of the way and close your eyes," Frances instructed and began to apply powder liberally. "We may have to powder your arms as well because you're so fair." Mary took a breath, coughed and waved a hand in front of her face.

"I just hope we don't put Joe in a compromising position or anything."

"Compromising position? Look here, he's put himself in a compromising position just being here. What kind of foolish spy job is he doing, anyway? He reminds me of Alex in a way, always rushing off to get in awful messes. Except that Alex is forever trying to turn a dollar, by hook or crook, they call it, while your old Joe's out to stir up some kind of trouble for that CIA outfit. That's why we have to keep an eye on them, dear, to keep them out of trouble and everything. Men must be managed; haven't you seen that by now? Showing them what's what is why we came on this trip in the first place."

Mary smiled, picked up the tube of hot pink lipstick, turned out a good quarter-inch and smeared it on her pursed lips. "How's that look?"

"Pretty good," Frances said with encouragement, "but rub a little rouge on your cheeks. We want to be authentic Cuban honeys, know what I mean." She inspected Mary's face in the mirror. "No wonder they say their men are hot blooded. We turn them on, don't we?"

Mary glanced at the mirror's reflection of Frances's lips, swiped broadly with red hot pink lipstick. "Do you really think we should do this?" They exchanged a brief stare. Then Frances grabbed the rum bottle and took Mary's arm.

"C'mon, girl, this is going to be the time of our lives."

In their new dresses, anyone in the lobby who saw them must assumed they were Rumba dancers there for Revolution Day entertainment. Escaping by the front door, Mary hailed a '57 Ford with a sign claiming "TAXI". They climbed in and realized they were not entirely sure where they were going.

"All I remember is it was near the waterfront," Frances said. "Seems like there were some ships down there."

With only a vague recollection, they told the driver to head south on any big street near the bay. Cedro, the driver, was happy to drive around anywhere. The problem was, as soon as they reached Carretera Casablanca the wide avenue was one huge traffic jam. They soon came to a complete stop.

"Everyone's in a hurry to get home and celebrate," he said. "It is always this way on Revolution Day." He shifted the old car into first and crawled along in the line of traffic.

"This is awful," Mary said. "We'll never be able to find Joe. We don't even know if it was him I saw."

"Of course, it was," Frances insisted, being slightly more tipsy on rum than Mary. "But there must be a better way."

Mary looked around for any way to go faster. Then when they stopped at the next light, she watched a rickshaw kind of thing cross in front of the cab. It was a bicycle with a two-seater kind of carriage in back. A teenaged boy pedaled it across and stopped at the corner. Mary pointed it out to Frances.

"Pull over, Dedro, Cedro, whatever your name is," Frances ordered. "We'll catch the Express." She leaned out of the window and shouted. "Hey, bike guy. Wait up! ARRET-TAY, HALT, ALTO. Yeah, you!"

Cedro let them out at the curb and Frances tossed a wad of pesos into the front seat and got out. He made change and tried to hand it to her.

"You keep it," she said. "It's all play money to me." She hustled toward the bicycle taxi. C'mon Mary." The two of them pulled up their ruffled skirts and climbed onto what looked like a converted loveseat attached behind the driver."

"*¿A dónde quieres ir?*" the boy asked.

"We don't know. Just go, thataway." She motioned straight ahead. "Go on. Mush!"

• CHAPTER THIRTEEN •

When Joe walked in the door of *EL ESCONDITE* with Marsha, he was hit with a barrage of raucous Spanish conversation and thick cigar smoke. Letting his eyes adjust to the dank dark interior, he scanned the room. Over in a corner to the left, he spotted Hosea seated in a booth waving to them. Across from Hosea sat a skeletal figure with dark eyes and unkempt hair. Maybe thirty-five or forty, Joe guessed, and clearly either sick or a rummie, maybe. The man had his bony fingers around a nearly empty shot glass and barely looked up. Joe pulled up a chair for Marsha, took the backpack off his shoulder and slipped in beside Hosea.

"Joe, this is Felipe Lopez. Felipe has many years as an engineer, right?" The guy hardly looked up until Hosea kicked his leg under the table. "Tell him about your experience, Lopez."

The drunk tried to focus on Joe. "Been fuckin' around diesels all my life," Felipe slurred. "Been in every goddam port you can think of—Rio to London—working my greasy ass off in stinking banana boats and oilers."

"Can you run big Caterpillar diesels?" Joe asked, feeling rather skeptical.

"Caterpillars, Weser, Abato, Accustar, GMT, Ajax, Akasaka, shit, man, you name it, I can fuck it." He turned the glass up to his mouth and chugged down its contents. Joe shook his head.

"Got any references?"

"References? Shit, yeah. How 'bout Ron Rico and Don Bacardi.

I'm a charter member of Havana Club. On the best of terms with all 'em. Even…" He picked up the bottle and squinted at it, trying to read the label. "Even this crap Hosea's bought." Hosea jerked the bottle out of his hand.

"How can you expect Señor Joe to hire you if you don't straighten up and talk some sense."

"Never mind," Joe interrupted as he stood up. "I think I'll pass on this one." He turned to walk away. Hosea jumped up and grabbed his arm.

"I can understand your objections, *señor*," he said. "But Felipe has been in crews from many countries. He knows his engines, I swear. He can manage far better than you think." Joe tried to imagine this man in the engine room and shook his head.

"Thanks, but I'm not that desperate," he said, and pulled away.

"I still need that favor, *compadre*," Hosea called after him. "I assure you we can make it all work. You'll see." Joe shook his head and motioned to Marsha to leave.

"It'll be a cold day in Habana," Joe replied on the way out.

When they stepped out to the street, Joe realized he had no place to go and no idea of what to do next. Marsha sensed he was utterly perplexed.

"I'd be very happy to let you stay a night or so at my place," she said. "Never mind about Maria. She's likely to find some *mano* to spend tonight with, don't you know, because this is a big holiday and everybody gets snockered. I mean everybody." She cozied up to him. "You and I could go get drunk, too."

Joe grimaced, recognizing the overtones of the invitation. He thought about Mary and how he had been unfaithful to her once before. A memory of his tryst in Northern Ireland with the ill-fated Fiona came to him. Was he not capable of being faithful? Were sexual encounters part of every agent's spy mission? He thought of waking up with Maria astride him. Perhaps one should just let things happen… *What kind of man are you?* he asked himself. He looked down at Marsha, who was clinging to him affectionately.

"So nice of you to invite me to stay, Marsha," he replied, nodding with a smile. "If it's not too much trouble, I'd love to have your sofa for the night." He thought but did not say how likely it might be for him to end up in a Cuban prison tomorrow.

"Just remember," she said, "When the time comes, I wanna go to the States with you." She stared at him until he nodded, then went off to the kitchen.

Joe sighed, realizing that sailing off on the ship was hard enough without having to figure out some way to get her aboard. That was one promise he just might not be able to keep.

Arm in arm, the two of them walked down the street toward her flat. Evening traffic was heavy on the main *avenida* as Havana's night people took to the streets, and the sounds of flamenco music competed with African salsa beats as rum-infused celebrants flooded the sidewalks.

"Is it always like this in your neighborhood?" he asked jokingly as they made their way between groups of revelers.

"It's worse on Revolution Day," she replied. "Such celebrating you've never seen. This is the one thing I will hate to leave. Oh, Joe. Do you really mean to take me back to Miami?" She reached out and took his hand. "I thought I was stranded here forever. Are you going to take me along? Are you?" Glancing down at their clasped hands, he recognized the desperation in her voice.

They pushed past two guitarists and a trumpeter surrounded by a knot of black and brown women doing the rhumba. Three men stood nearby, ogling the dancers, apparently selecting partners for the night. As they went on past, Joe worried how he could refuse to take her, even though it would be exposing her to extreme peril to do so. As they walked along, he leaned over and spoke gently.

"Listen, Marsha. You don't know who I am. What I'm doing is… well I don't know how dangerous…"

"Dangerous?" she repeated, and he felt her grip loosen slightly. "You don't strike me as somebody who's in any rough stuff. I mean, you're one of those who avoids trouble, right?" She tightened her grip on his hand again. "I don't care, of course, but where I grew up, all the guys were in street gangs, know what I mean, and so I guess you're different."

He was about to reply with the explanation that he had just been putting on an act to ward off her lascivious roommate Maria. While Marsha droned on about how she was very broadminded about LGBT's and such, he focused instead on an odd-looking bicycle taxi ahead. It was not the vehicle but its passengers. A couple of fairer-skinned women in gaudy low-cut, ruffled dresses were strangely familiar.

"Did you hear me, Joe?" Marsha said, still holding onto his arm. "I was trying to tell you I'm ready for anything." Joe nodded but was still staring at the bicycle taxi. One of the women had red hair and the other was blonde. The redhead was older. Then the terrifically familiar looking blonde turned toward him, and he nearly collapsed in shock.

• CHAPTER FOURTEEN •

"There's Joe!" Frances cried. "It is that sorry so and so, standing there holding hands with some Cuban hussy right here in front of us." She leaned forward and slapped the bicycler on the back. "Whoa! Whoa! *Arretezi, alto,* whatever." He steered over to the sidewalk and stopped, then reached around to touch his back where she slapped.

Mary jumped to the sidewalk and nearly fell down. Frances staggered off the other side. Charging through a small crowd of noisily celebrating Cubans, Mary rushed toward Joe but stopped a few feet away, realizing Marsha was still holding his arm.

"Mary!" he cried. "It IS you!" He pulled away from Marsha and rushed over to embrace her. "What? How the hell?" She embraced him for an instant, glanced at Marsha, and stepped back from him, just as Frances lurched up.

"I thought we'd find you down here in this slummy part of town," Frances said, "and you've already got your hands on a Cuban hussy, have you?"

"Just a minute, sweetie face," Marsha said. "I ain't no hussy, and I sure ain't Cuban. So who the hell are you in that ridiculous Latin whore's outfit?"

Frances was raring back, mustering up apt invective, when the bicycler taxi boy interrupted.

"Mi fuego es de quince pesos, por favor." No one even heard him.

"Oh, Mary, wait. What?" Joe tried to hug her again. She pulled away. "Where? How did you two get here?" Joe demanded. He was as incensed as she was. Mary burst into tears.

Joe hugged her tightly. "Mary, don't you know I love you."

"*Quince pesos,*" the boy insisted loudly. "*Xiao, llamo policia?*"

"No. no. No police! *No llames a la policia,*" Joe reached for his wallet and pulled out a twenty peso bill. "*Dejame pagarte.*" He handed over the money, and the boy smiled and left. Joe turned back to Mary. She collected herself.

"We came on a tour," Mary said while she dried her eyes. "I didn't know you were here."

"Did the tour make you wear those silly dresses?" Marsha asked. "I've been in Cuba for years and never had the nerve to wear something like that."

"This is Marsha," Joe explained. "She has been a great help to me."

"Yeah, 'help' huh?" Frances said. "You ought to know better," Frances complained, her voice getting louder and louder. "A man your age with another woman, and she's not half as pretty as Mary. You ought to be ashamed, coming down here to Cuba pretending that you're on some kind of spy mission for the CIA. And it was all about having more women. I tell you what."

Joe was about to tell her to shut up when he noticed a police car coming slowly and stopping nearby in the heavy traffic. The windows were rolled down, and the policemen scanned the crowds as if looking for someone. Joe turned so as to hide his face until the car passed on by.

"Frances, please!" Joe pleaded, putting his hand up to stop her. He noticed that the musicians on the corner had stopped playing and were gawking at them mirthfully. "Quiet down, please. I'll explain…"

"Explain? How can you explain away another woman?" Frances went on, pointing accusingly at Marsha.

"Joe, who are these women?" Marsha demanded.

Joe put out his arms and herded the three ladies away, motioning for everyone to please be quiet. He looked at Mary, pleading.

"Mary, this is Marsha. I'll explain. Marsha, this is my girlfriend, Mary, and our friend, Frances."

"Maybe I'm not your GIRLFRIEND," Mary announced angrily.

"I thought you were here in Cuba alone, Joe," Marsha said.

"I am. I mean, I was. Uh, look, I can explain…" He was as desperate as he was confused. "Marsha, can we go to your apartment and…"

"See, he knows about her apartment," Frances said, pointing an accusing finger. "I told you, men can't be trusted. If Alex were here, why, I guess he'd have two women on his arms. That's the way he…"

"Excuse me, Señor," a man from the crowd with a strong breath of alcohol spoke up behind them, waving a rum bottle. "An hombre with three women may need another mano to join your fun, savvy?" He leered at Mary, winked and laughed. The musicians and the crowd had surrounded them. The one with the trumpet tooted a lewd kind of wail. Everyone laughed. Joe saw the police car slowing down to observe the gathering.

"C'mon, we've got to go now," Joe said. He put his arms out to separate the ladies from the crowd and tried to herd them on. "This way, please, quick. Let's go."

Mary gave him an unhappy and skeptical look but acquiesced to his urgings.

"It's just down the street," Marsha said. "We can sort it all out there."

"Thanks," Joe said, urging them on as fast as he could, thinking that Marsha's place would provide momentary safety. His head was spinning. What in the world were Mary and Frances doing there? What in heavens name was he going to do about the ship? He didn't have a mechanic; he didn't have a good plan; he didn't have a clue.

Marsha led them off the street and up the stairs, leaving the din of celebration below. Joe was trying to hurry Mary and Frances along in front of him, but the two were inebriated enough to stumble a bit on the steps. From Mary's severe glances at him, Joe could tell that she was not convinced about his innocent relationship with Marsha. Well, he was upset with Mary, too. The very idea of coming to interfere with his mission in Cuba! Of course, he loved Mary very much, even if he was mad as hell at her for being here. But the situation at hand was dire, to say the least, and he knew his keeping a lid on things was important to everyone's survival. He pulled her aside.

"I'm going to explain when I get a chance," he whispered to her. "Right now, we've just got to figure out what to do."

"I'm waiting for that," she replied.

"Look, there's a ship in the harbor that belongs to CIA," Joe said in her ear. "It's a long story, but I have to sneak on board and take it to sea."

"What?" Mary looked astounded. "Not a boat? What kind of boat."

"A ship, dammit, a ship! Three hundred feet or so, twenty-five hundred tons, filled with electronics gear, oh yeah, and big load of rum to boot."

"And you're supposed to take the ship to sea?" She looked at him as if he were insane. "It sounds impossible to me. How, Joe? How could you? I mean it just sounds absurd, ridiculous, crazy."

Joe shook his head. "Maybe not, but… Well, I can't say more right now. Keep it to yourself."

Mary shivered. "Why would you do this?"

"Why? And what are you and Frances doing here, and in these get-ups?" He let out his breath in exasperation. "Wait 'til we get inside the apartment."

As they reached the landing, they could hear music coming from inside. When Marsha unlocked the door, they all went in. The old television was on, showing scenes of carnival goers in the street. Then Maria came out of the bedroom.

"*Hola. Que sorpresa*! Who are these women?"

"Joe's friends," Marsha said, as she went to the TV and turned down the volume. "I thought you would be out on the town, celebrating." She looked at Maria apologetically. Joe grimaced, desperate to explain everything to Mary and Frances and somehow get them back to their tour group. He needed to concoct a plan, but how could he discuss anything in front of Maria?

"Americanos?" Maria guessed, looking at Mary and Frances? "Strange to see you on your own here. I hear your *Presidenta* doesn't allow Americans to wander around Cuba." She sucked in her breath and pointed at them and backed up a step. "You must be spies, no?"

"If they are Joe's friends, they are our friends, okay?" Marsha said. "One way or the other, it's not our business, Maria." The two roommates stared at one another a moment, and then Maria shrugged her shoulders.

"There are many people around who like to report things to the police," Maria said. "It pays for the government to consider you an informer." She gave an impish grin. "Of course, you can bribe anyone. Life is not easy, you know."

Joe was considering how he was going to shut her up. Judging by the way Maria had climbed into bed with him, he supposed she was capable of anything. He looked at Marsha. She returned his gaze, realized what he was thinking and gasped.

"She's a good kid, really, she is." She turned toward her roommate. "Aren't you, Maria?" Then she looked at Joe again. "Maybe she could... I don't know." They stood staring at one another in a momentary silence. The sound of music from the television suddenly was interrupted by an announcement, "*Atención, Atención! Personas desaparecidas.*"

"Look!" Mary exclaimed. "The TV. It's us!" Joe glanced at the television and nearly choked. The newscaster was announcing that two tourists were missing, and on the screen were passport photos of Frances and Mary. They listened in shocked silence.

"*Faltan dos mujeres americanas*," they heard. "*Ausentes del tour*. Two American women from Gala Tours are missing. They were last seen at four in the afternoon, going to their room in Hotel Havana. They did not appear for the scheduled cocktail party, and their tour guide cannot locate them." The announcer went on to give a brief description of Mary and Frances, requesting that anyone who sees them should contact the police. Joe gave Mary a look of disapproval.

"Why are you in trouble, Mary? Did you break the rules?"

"Our tour guide said we were not to go anywhere on our own, but Frances and I thought we could sneak out a couple of hours and no one would know."

"If you, Joe Anderson, hadn't been down here in the first place," Frances countered, "we wouldn't have seen you wandering the streets, consorting with women, playing James Bond and making Mary want to go find you. What are you up to, anyway, you ole devil? Seems to me you're always stirring up something."

Joe had tuned her out. He was thinking hard about what to do next. Then Maria captured his attention. She was shaking her finger at them.

"And so you are spies in our homeland, *si*?" She glared at Joe. "And you must be a spy, too? I wondered why you were here so strange-like." She gasped, looked at Marsha, and blurted out, "we have to tell the *policia*!" With that she started for the door. Joe bolted toward her. Marsha was closer and grabbed Maria's arm. Maria let out a yelp and tried to break free.

"Wait, Maria, hush," Marsha said. "They are our friends. We…" Maria struggled to get free, but Marsha hung on. "Joe is going to take me home, Maria. He's going to get me back to the States. I need his help, please listen."

"See, Mary," Frances said. "I knew it. I knew if he got down here by himself, he'd chase another woman just like Alex would. I tell you what, men can't be trusted. Here you are, letting this man live with you, and all he wants to do is go on these silly missions for CIA and get all embroiled with other women."

"That is so wrong," Joe said. "How can you accuse me like that?"

"Wait, Frances," Mary interrupted. "Let Joe tell us what he has to do with…"

"I love you, Mary. You know that, of course you do."

Marsha and Maria had ceased to struggle, looking at the others with curious surprise.

"I thought you were gay," Maria said. "You acted like you were gay. When I found you here, all naked in the bed. How could you have not… "

"Naked in bed! Aha!" Frances said. "See Mary, I told you…"

Marsha had let go of her roommate. "So you were just pretending? It was to…"

"Make me look the fool," Maria cried. She started for the door again. "So you still are a spy, illegal in our country. I will go and report you—all of you."

Marsha took Maria's arm. "But you can go, too, Maria. You can go to America, can't she Joe? Think of how you've told me before how great it would be to join your cousins in Miami, get a real job, see the country. I'll take you to New York. Just think about New York, Maria."

"If I had the choice of going to New York or staying here in this wild commie country," Frances said, "I know what I'd do."

Maria paused an instant, looking around at them. Then with a little yelp, she raced for the door. Joe was there in two leaps, cutting her off. He grabbed her right arm and stepped behind, putting her in an armlock. She screamed, and he slammed his hand over her mouth. The other women gasped.

"Get something to tie her up, quick. A sheet off the bed, some tape, anything," Joe shouted. He was trying hard not to hurt her, but he had to keep her quiet. "Marsha, do it!" Maria squirmed and managed to kick Joe in the shin. He winced and pulled her around to the sofa and threw her down, putting his knee on her legs. She groaned and sat motionless, her teary eyes blazing anger.

"I don't want to hurt you, really I don't," Joe said. "But just be still, okay."

"The *policia* will come and they will HURT you," she retorted. "You are the one in trouble."

Marsha appeared out of the bedroom with a sheet from the bed all bundled up in her arms. Joe motioned for her to bring it over to him. She paused and then did so, saying, "I don't want you to harm her, Joe. Maria's always lived in Cuba. She doesn't know anything different. That's why she's afraid of the idea of leaving." She smiled at her friend. "I have to go home, Maria dear. You would like it in the States."

"We will take care of you there," Mary said. She went over behind Maria and put a hand on her shoulder. "We'd help you get established and everything." Clearly, Mary had sobered quite a bit. "Can't we just calm down and talk a minute." It seemed to settle Maria somewhat. She looked quizzically at Joe.

"And so Señor Spy, how do you plan to get everyone away from Cuba?"

Joe thought to himself that he wished he knew. "I have a way, but I'm certainly not going to tell you." He reached down to his ankle and pulled the pistol out of its holster. Maria screamed and struggled to get free. Joe restrained her and then handed the gun to Mary.

"If she moves or starts shouting, shoot her," he said, secretly winking at Mary. She hesitated and then gingerly took the weapon, apparently realizing that the bluff was enough to restrain the girl.

"Good thing you didn't hand the pistol to me," Frances said, wanting in on the act. She pointed her finger at Maria. "I'd shoot in a second."

Joe grimaced. Recalling Frances aboard *Mission* firing her pistol at the pirates, he was certain she meant every word of it.

"Everybody just sit tight," he commanded. He headed for the kitchen. "I need to make a call."

• CHAPTER FIFTEEN •

"Where is my engineer?" Standing in Marsha's kitchen to have some privacy, it was all he could do to keep from shouting in his phone, but he didn't want the women to hear, especially not Maria.

"We've found a guy," Adams said. "It's going to take a few days to get him up to speed and then get him down there."

"I haven't got a few days, dammit." Joe now was shouting into his phone. "I've got some real problems here." He stopped himself from telling his handler that Mary and Frances were there. For one thing, they weren't supposed to know that Joe was in Cuba. He realized there was nothing Adams could do for him now.

"We can't just ship this guy down there without training or anything…"

"Forget the frigging engineer," Joe cut him off. "I haven't got time for all that. I'm going tonight."

"That's stupid, Anderson," Adams said. "I order you to wait until I can…"

"I can't wait, dammit! Among other stings there's a girl here that's ready to tell the police about me."

"Can't stay away from the women, can you? I recall your getting mixed up with one in Northern Ireland, and look what happened," Adams said.

A great sense of nausea coursed through Joe as the memory of Fiona flashed through his mind.

"That was different," he countered. "I ran into this woman by accident. She... Well, fuck you, anyway!"

"You need to do away with her," the handler said calmly, "if your mission is threatened." Joe froze in disbelief.

"What? Kill her? Is that what you're saying?" He was truly sickened now.

"Your mission comes first, Anderson. Your duty to your country. Don't ever forget that."

"Yeah, and whatever happened to morality and common decency? You CIA stiffs make me sick."

"Look, you've put your whole life on the line, taking this job. If this... woman gets you arrested by the Cubans, you'll either be shot as a spy or rot in one of their prisons for a very long time. I hear that dengue fever is the first thing that happens, and then who knows what's next—malaria?" There was a long silence.

"I'm coming tonight," Joe said finally. "So be ready."

"And how can you possibly get the ship underway without someone to operate the engine for you?"

"I'll work something out. Just get the coast guard or navy or whatever to meet me beyond the twelve-mile limit. I'll be there in the morning." He inwardly yelled at himself, *How the shit are you going to do that?*

"I'll see what I can do," Adams replied. "Remember one thing. If you're not out there when they arrive, it'll be mighty hard to get them to come back on another day."

"There won't be another day," Joe said. The appearance of Mary and Frances with the police searching for them had created an impossible crisis. "It's now or never."

"Wish I could help you, sport," Adams said. "Not much else I can do."

"Just get a destroyer or a frigate or a friggin' rowboat to meet me. I'll manage to get out to sea somehow. It's gonna happen tonight, before dawn, one way or the other." There was a pause before Adams replied.

"It's your call. Cowboy. Whatever you say."

"Damn right it is," Joe said. He clicked off his phone and slammed it against his hand. He had only half an idea about what to do. But one thing was certain. He had to get Mary and Frances out of Cuba before the police found them. Why did they have to come here? Never mind. No point in dwelling on that.

What to do with Maria? He peered through the doorway at the women still surrounding the Cuban girl. Their efforts to convince her to go with them did not seem to be working. All logic and CIA training told him that she would have to be neutralized in some way, even if it meant taking her out permanently.

The memory came to him of lovely Fiona lying on the floor, bleeding to death from the bullet wound of her brother's pistol. He shivered and forced the thought from his mind. As desperate as the situation was, Marsha wouldn't stand for any violence to her roommate, nor would Mary and Frances. Nor would he himself for that matter. There had to be another way to handle Maria.

He looked around the kitchen and spotted a closet door. He opened it and found it had just enough room for her if he took out a broom, and mop and bucket and some boxes of things. He went out to join the ladies.

"Maria, I can do this gently, or I can make it just as painful as you want. But we're going to tie you up." He picked up the sheet and tore off a long strip. "Stand up and put your hands behind you." He glanced at Mary. She was still pointing the gun at the girl. Maria looked imploringly at Marsha, who only shrugged and shook her head.

"What will you do with me?" Maria cried.

"You're going to get to know that kitchen closet very well," Joe said. He wrapped the piece of sheet around her left wrist and tied it as best he could. Then as he put her right hand in the other side and tied it, he could not help but remember their intimate moments on the bed. Well, she had taken advantage of his drunken stupor—raped him if you wanted to think of it that way. He knew that wasn't true; a man of his experience certainly isn't the subject of rape, anyway. Then he focused back on the current problem. These knots in a sheet wouldn't hold for long, not with a lot of struggling going on. He pushed her down on the sofa and tied her legs together."

"Now let's get her in the closet." He lifted her up in his arms and started for the kitchen.

"What about gagging her?" Mary asked tentatively. "Oh, I hope not."

"Maybe we can just turn the TV up," Marsha suggested. "There's so much noise out on the street with everybody celebrating. I doubt anyone will hear her."

"Wait," Mary said, just as Joe was about to put Maria down in the closet. "Let's put her in a chair." She pulled over a wooden table chair. Joe nodded, and Mary set it inside. A snug fit but okay. He put her down in the seat.

"Please! I cannot stand this!" Maria cried.

"I can't help it," Joe said. "Under the circumstances, you're getting out pretty light." He shut the door and pulled the dining table over in front of it. She already was kicking at the door.

"That's not going to hold her very long," Mary said.

"Maybe an hour or so, which should be long enough. She doesn't know where we're going."

"To the harbor, I'll bet," Frances said. "You must have a boat..."

"Shhh. Shut up!" Joe said, motioning them toward the livingroom. He glanced at the door. Had Maria heard? He surely hoped not. Well, they had precious little time to cobble some kind of escape plan to-gether, so they might as well get with it.

He gathered the four of them in the living room. Mary gingerly handed Joe the pistol, which he stuck in his ankle holster. She clearly was very worried. Frances, however, just gave an inebriated smirk. Marsha was trying to gather up a few belongings.

"No way, Marsha. You can't take anything," he said. "Listen ladies, we are in extremis, understand? We've got one shot at escape. So listen carefully."

He looked at Mary and Frances, both still in their costumes, and sighed deeply.

"I have to go to *EL ESCONDITE* to find someone," he explained.

"Oh no," Marsha exclaimed. "Not for that guy!"

"What choice do we have?"

"What are you all talking about?" Mary asked.

"Never mind, just go," Joe said. "The three of you need to head directly down to the docks. Marsha knows where." He dropped his voice nearly to a whisper to keep Maria from hearing. "Marsha, you do know it's the *Sea Urchin*, the one just forward of that Russian freighter?"

"Oh, yeah. I've seen it. The one with the guards on the dock."

"That's it. Everybody, just act like you're celebrating like everyone else, all right?"

"I've been celebratin' since four o'clock," Frances interjected. Joe glanced at her with irritation and shook his head.

"Never mind! Look, Marsha, have you got any liquor?"

"Of course. You don't think I could live in Cuba being sober all the time."

"Okay, good. Everybody take along a bottle of something. Dance and sing or whatever along the way. Wait for me at the corner of the warehouses across from the ship. There's an armed guard at the ship's gangway. For God's sake, stay away from him until I get there. I'll be there quick as I can."

"That's your plan?" Frances asked sarcastically. "Remind me not to call on you for…"

"Never mind, Frances, for goodness sakes," Mary said. "Let's just go."

Marsha took one last look around. "Funny how there's really nothing here I want to take with me," she said. "Come on. New York, here I come."

Joe smiled thinly. "As he followed them out the door, instructing Marsha to lock it, he felt terribly unprepared for whatever was about to come.

"Lord, help us," he said. He grabbed Mary in a quick, less-than-tender embrace. "Take care, all of you. I'll meet you at the ship. It's the *Sea Urchin*."

They nodded and watched as Joe hurried on down the steps, going ahead. He sprinted as best he could through the crowds of celebrants on the street. Apparently, anyone not outside with a bottle of rum and a song on their lips wasn't with Revolution Day. As he nearly stumbled over people in his haste, Joe hoped desperately that Hosea's mechanic would still be at the bar and would be sober enough to go start up the ship's engine. If not, Joe would have to do it himself, and that likely would be a fiasco of the first order.

. . .

THE MUSIC, THE CIGAR smoke, the smell of rum and sweaty people engulfed him once again as he entered *EL ESCONDITE*. Through the crowd he saw Hosea at the bar, talking earnestly to some men. He spotted Joe immediately as if he had been waiting for him, and made his way over. Even in the dim light, Joe could see on his face the anxious look of a man who wanted something. *The favor*, Joe guessed, whatever it was.

"I hoped you'd be back, Señor Joe."

"Where's Lopez, your so-called mechanic?" Joe shouted above the din of Revolution Day celebrating. Hosea pointed toward the booth where the three of them met earlier and led the way over.

They made their way through the crowd of drinkers, most of whom were falling-down drunk themselves. Felipe Lopez was blotto, passed out where Joe had left him a couple of hours ago. Joe grabbed the sot by the arm and shook him but got no more than a grunt. The guy was still alive at least. Joe made his way to the bar, finally got the bartenders attention and ordered a pitcher of ice water. As he was paying, he spotted a half-full bottle of Havana Club, and asked the man to top it off with water. Then he went back to Hosea's so-called engineer and poured half the ice water on his head. Felipe jerked violently and sat up, trying to focus on Joe. Joe splashed more ice water in his face.

"Get up," he shouted. "I need you now." The Cuban wrinkled his nose, trying to see Joe through the daze. Joe shot a look around. The place was so crowded, smoke-filled, and boisterous no one would see or care what he did to the drunken man. Joe splashed the rest of the water on the Cuban's face and then pulled on his arm.

"A thousand pesos if you come right now," he said and dangled the Havana Club bottle in front of him. "A thousand pesos and all the rum you can drink, *sabe*?" Felipe shivered a bit and groaned. Joe grabbed a hand full of money from his pocket and waved it in front of the man.

"Lots of pesos, *comprende*? *Mucho dinero, mucho.*" He grabbed him by the arm and pulled him up. "Let's go, dammit, let's go."

As if both the bills and the bottle were magnets, Felipe managed to drag himself out of the seat and stand. With Hosea's help, Joe reached under his arm and half escorted, half dragged the man to the door. By the time they reached the front door, Felipe was staggering but walking, at least. They went outside and let the drunk take in a few gasps of fresh air.

"He'll be okay," Hosea said. "An hombre who drinks that much does better drunk." He grabbed Joe's hand. "Now, *amigo*, I need you to be ready to help me. The favor, remember?"

"Look," Joe said, withdrawing his hand. "I have no time for anything, *comprende?* This alcoholic wonder and I have got all we can handle."

"Nothing for you to do, Joe," Hosea said. "Just let me do what I need. *Me permit, eso es todo."*

"I'm in a fucking big hurry," Joe said. "So just don't get in my way, got it?"

Felipe and Joe exchanged stares, and Hosea nodded.

"*Entiendo.*" Hosea trotted away. "*Asta la vista,*" he called back. "*Buena suerte*"

"Damn right," Felipe slurred. At least he could walk and talk.

Turning his attention to the mechanic, Joe not too gently pushed him in the direction of the docks. Thanks to Hosea, he had a mechanic now, an engineer, by damn, and this guy was going to perform or be keelhauled under the ship all the way to Miami. Somehow it was going to happen or this guy was going to be dead, or maybe it would be both of them.

Now, for God's sake, he wondered. *Where are the ladies?*

• CHAPTER SIXTEEN •

The sidewalk along the *avenida* was even more crowded than before. Above the din of celebration, there was a distant rumble of thunder, but no one except Mary seemed to notice. To her it seemed the entire neighborhood was out in the warm night air to dance and drink. She, Frances, and Marsha made their way through the crowds as best they could. Then they encountered the same musicians that had accosted them before.

"So you are back, no?" the trumpeter said. "*Ven a clebrar la revolución.*" He and the man with the guitar and the other with a bongo drum began circling as they banged out another stanza of "*Viva Castro.*" Marsha and Mary tried to push on by, but Frances picked up her skirt to perform a couple of rhumba steps before catching up.

"Frances, don't encourage them," Mary whispered, but to no avail. Even though many of the Cuban women were similarly dressed in ruffled skirts, the trio of fair-skinned ladies apparently seemed unusual and thus attractive to the musicians, and they began to follow. The guitar player trotted up beside Mary.

"*Buenas noches, bella dama. Mi nombre es Jesús.* I think you are the prettiest one I have seen tonight," he said, stepping in front of her. Mary sidestepped and walked faster.

"We are in a hurry," she said in her poor attempt at Spanish. They pushed on through a little group of people, but the man persisted.

"Ah, *extranjero,*" he guessed. "A foreigner, *Americana* perhaps?" Mary shook her head and motioned frantically to Frances to hurry along. The other music makers flanked her, however, still playing. Jesus, the drummer joined in, making eyes at Mary all the while. She looked at Marsha for guidance.

"In Brooklyn, I'd tell him to fuck off," Marsha said. "It doesn't work here. They take it literally and just get more encouraged."

"If we were in Birmingham," Frances said, "I'd have my pistol out. That works anywhere."

"*Ah Pistola?*" the Cuban said. "*Tengo un pene no una pistola, no?*" The drummer and the trumpeter laughed uproariously.

"What'd he say?" Frances asked. Marsha gave her a little push to move on.

"He said he has a penis, not a pistol," she explained. "Just keep walking." They picked up the pace.

"Let's tell them we're going to meet our husbands," Mary suggested. She looked at Jesus. "*Ir a conocer a nuestros…uh husbands…* Uh, how do you say…*maridos.*" The bongo player grinned at her and shrugged.

"*Si, bella dama,*" he said and reached for the bottle in Marsha's hand.

"That won't deter anyone here in Cuba," Marsha advised, as she jerked back the quart of rum she had brought from the apartment. "They seem to condone extracurriculars. Just keep walking." Mary let out her breath in desperation.

"Whatever will we do if they go all the way to the harbor with us?"

"We need to think of something," Marsha agreed. But Frances grabbed both their arms and stopped.

"Say, I have an idea." Frances produced a handful of pesos, fanned them out and showed them to the musicians. "Come on, you amigos you. We're gonna put on a party!"

• • •

As if trying to entice a mule with a feedbag and a whip, Joe alternated between encouraging his new mechanic with the promise of

many pesos and telling him he would beat the crap out of him if he
didn't sober up.

"Take it easy, man," Felipe slurred., careening into the brick wall
beside them, and beginning to slump down. "Just gimme a little nip
from that bottle you're carrying."

Joe snatched the bottle away, reached down to his ankle holster
and jerked out the pistol.

"I don't want you to have any doubts about how serious I am," he
warned. "Now get your sorry ass UP!" Felipe's eyes widened, and he
stood up, palms out toward Joe.

"I'm with ya, okay? Don't worry. Jesus! You're a mean fucker."

"I can get a lot meaner," Joe threatened. "You just better be able
to get that engine running, you hear me?"

"Listen, man, I can do it, okay? You'll see. I'm telling you…"

Joe shoved him on. "Shut up. No promises. All I want is your best
friggin' effort, and not another word till we get there."

Distant thunder caused Joe to look up at the sky. A storm was
coming, but that was the least of his worries. He had told the ladies
to meet him at the corner across the quay from the ship, but he had
a rather poor idea of what to do when they all got there. All he had
was his pistol.

That morning, after his long conversation with the old guard at
the ship, he had overheard him speaking to a younger soldier, who
demanded Hermano take the duty tonight. Joe hoped his acquaintance
with Hermano would cause the old soldier to be off his guard and
therefore easier to deal with. Maybe he could trick the fellow somehow.
But if not, then suppose he actually had to shoot the old man? The
thought was repugnant to say the least. Now, however, he had Mary
to think of—Mary and Frances and Marsha had to be protected at all
cost, and protecting them overrode any other humanitarian concerns.

Still, the whole idea was making him feel sick at his stomach, and he prayed that somehow some miracle might happen.

Fortunately, the drunken Felipe was walking steadily enough without complaint. Lightning from the approaching thunderstorm occasionally lit the darkened roadway to the piers. About half a block from the harbor, they could hear the bongo beat and blare of trumpet ahead. As they rounded the corner, Joe was amazed to see people dancing to mambo music. And then he realized that it was Mary, Frances and Marsha, along with three musicians gathered just outside the sentry's tent. Hermano was standing there with his rifle slung on his shoulder watching them. Astounded, Joe caught hold of Felipe to stop him. They paused and watched the spectacle. Frances, who still had quite a figure for her age, was holding up her skirt in can-can fashion. As if she performed on stage every day, Frances danced over to Hermano and took his hand.

"Hey, man. A party!" the mechanic slurred with a yuk. In disbelief, Joe sucked in his breath.

"Let's go see," he said. Stuffing the pistol in his right pants pocket where it would be reachable more quickly, Joe then shoved Felipe ahead.

When the women saw Joe and his captive coming, they waved with unexpected, unwarranted gaiety. Surprised, Joe felt he was watching some sort of theater production.

"Oh, good, you're here," Mary said when the music ended. She affected a big smile. "We're celebrating the Revolution."

"Did you bring more rum?" Marsha asked. "God, I hope so."

The guard appeared amused at the revelers, but then he warily eyed Joe and the sotted mechanic. Joe nodded to the soldier like an old friend.

"*Buenas noches, Señor Hermano, mi amigo,*" he said. "I hope my friends are not disturbing you."

"*Tus amigas? Americanas?*" he asked. "Where does a Canadian find American women in Havana?" He still had his very formidable Kalashnikov strapped on his shoulder and looked at Joe with growing suspicion. "And where did you find this drunk? He is well known around here for his worthlessness."

"We are all friends on Revolution Day," Joe said, attempting an air of casualness. "And my innebriated friend, this *hombre está borracho*, followed me from some bar. I guess he saw what I was carrying." Joe opened the bag and pulled out two bottles of Ron Rico. Felipe reached for one but Joe brushed his hand away, making him stagger. The trumpet player laughed.

"*Mucho ebrio, no?*" The guitar player strummed a few minor notes.

Joe flamboyantly ripped off the cap of the first bottle and started to pass it around.

"*Las damas primero*, ladies first," Frances said and took the bottle from him with a dramatic flourish. She drank a big gulp as if she did that every day. As Marsha and Mary applauded, Frances held it out to Hermano.

"Aw, c'mon. It's a special night, after all." Hermano paused, noticing everyone was waiting in anticipation.

"No need to be left out," Joe urged. The soldier shrugged, took a big swig, smiled and passed the bottle back. Felipe reached for it. Joe allowed him to have some but grabbed it back after the sot had two swallows. He held up the bottle to inspect it.

"We're going to need some more rum." Joe looked at the guard. "I heard this ship had a load of rum aboard."

Hermano glanced up at Joe. "Who told you about the rum, senór?" Joe grimaced.

"Oh, well, scuttlebutt around the docks. Just a rumor; *solo un rumor, no?*"

"*Carga de ron?*" Felipe perked up. His expression caused Hermano to smile.

"We can't let all that rum go to waste," Mary said, now in her full acting mode, "Shouldn't we go see? And besides, where can we find some drinking glasses." She looked at Hermano expectantly. He shrugged and shook his head.

"We must have glasses," Frances said, rather obviously repeating a rehearsed line. "Now where can we find glasses?"

"*Ahora dónde encontramos vasos,*" Joe translated.

Mary looked up at the deck of *Sea Urchin*. "On the ship!" she said with the sweep of her arm. "Surely there will be glasses, uh, *vasos* on the ship."

"*Y ron!*" Felipe added. Lightning flashed nearby and he staggered around to look. "*Viene una tormenta eléctrica.*"

"Ooh, let's take cover on the ship," she said. "Let's go. She grabbed the inebriated mechanic and took his arm. "C'mon *amigo. Ven conmigo.*" She led him toward the gangway. Mary grabbed Marsha's hand and they followed. Mary rhumbaed a couple of steps and motioned to the trumpet player.

"Music, Come make more music, *por favor*, And free booze, too. Let's go. Take the party to the ship."

In amazement Joe watched the spectacle of Mary, Frances, Marsha, the staggering Felipe, and the three raucously laughing musicians climbing the gangway stairs. By sheer gall they now were aboard the ship! He looked at Hermano and saw an expression of half astonishment, half amusement. Masking his own surprise as best he could, Joe grinned and shrugged.

"Shall we follow the ladies? They are so full of rum and celebration," he said, trying to affect an air of *alegria de vivir.* Their eyes met for a very long two seconds as the guard's expression darkened.

"*Espere un momento.* I am not sure..." Hermano said, tentatively, looking around to see who might be watching.

"No one could care," Joe assured him. "Everyone is celebrating. What harm can be done? *Viva la revolución!*" With a big smile and the sincere belief that he was about to be shot and killed, Joe made a gesture of resignation and went for the gangway. He started up the stairs and glanced back. He was amazed to see Hermano following, thankfully with his AK 47 still slung to his shoulder. All but in a daze from pumping adrenaline, Joe realized he didn't know what to do next. Here they were climbing aboard this ship with no idea of how to sail it out of there. And right behind him came an armed guard whose duty was to prevent any such thing happening.

On deck the women were rocking to trumpet and guitar, the only illumination coming from streetlights on the pier below and an occasional lightning flash. The bongo player had disappeared, but in a few minutes he came out of a hatch with two bottles. The musicians soon were playing and passing a bottle around. Hermano silently looked on from the top of the gangway, his face alternately showing amusement and concern. Frances and Marsha danced over to him, encouraging him as if he were an old friend.

"*Baila conmigo!* Dance with me, you old devil," Frances exclaimed and grabbed his arm. "Put that gun down and come on." With a broad sexy smile, she gently tried to pull the rifle sling off his shoulder, but he resisted politely. She faked a big laugh, grabbed him in an embrace and got him dancing. Marsha and Mary clapped as the musicians kept up the mambo beat, still passing the bottle.

Now what? Joe hardly could believe what had happened. The women had managed somehow to get them all on the ship. Of course, the engines hadn't been started, and only this stranger, Felipe, had any hope of getting them going. Even then *Sea Urchin* still would be moored to the pier. He watched the three musicians start up a new song. He watched Frances play her magic allure on Hermano.

Well, whatever was going to be done, Joe told himself, it had to be done now. It was a crazy situation and called for some insane action, that's all. He looked at Mary, his dearest Mary. If he failed, would she be arrested? Killed? He pulled her to him in an embrace. She responded with a desperate hug.

"What do we do?" she whispered. Joe held her tightly. He had to depend upon her to be her bravest. He recalled how wonderfully she had reacted to the dangers before. Now she would have to perform again. He pulled her aside.

"When you can slip away, walk along the starboard side and release all the mooring lines." She grimaced and looked at him skeptically.

"Just let the lines go—all six of them. Just undo them from the bits and drop the ends in the water. And do it as quick as you can."

"You mean just let the ship drift?" she said in surprise.

Joe shushed her. "The way the wind is out of the south and the tide is beginning to ebb," he whispered, "I hope it will take us out into the channel. If not, at least we'll be away from the dock while we get the engine going."

"With that drunken guy? How can he start the engine?" she asked with a frightened expression.

"I guess we're going to find out."

"Well, if you can't, and we drift off into the harbor," she paled as she spoke. "Then what?"

"Hell, I don't know." He pulled out his Glock pistol and tried to hand it to her. She shrank back.

"I can't take that."

"Yes, you can," he insisted and pressed it into her hand. "For protection, in case..." He paused. "But for God's sake, try not to shoot anybody, okay? I mean…" He stared at her, then kissed her cheek. "Just let loose the mooring lines. And take Marsha to help if you need to. But go on, go." He gave her a gentle push.

Mary gave him a look of panic, nodded and reluctantly headed off. Joe watched her take Marsha aside, whisper to her and then lead her away. Joe turned then to watch Frances with amazed admiration. She was all but embracing Hermano, still dancing, engaging him, displaying her genius as a manipulator. No question but she was playing her ad lib role perfectly.

"C'mon, you old sexy dog, you. Let's celebrate." She wrapped her arm around his shoulders and put the rum bottle to his lips. "*Viva la Revolution*," she slurred. "Let's dance." With a big smile on his face, the old soldier wiped the drool of rum from his chin and raised his arms for the waltz.

"Wait, you old devil," Frances said. "It's time you took silly gun off your shoulder. You can't dance with that sorry thing on." She reached over, took the strap and pulled it off." He resisted for an instant, shrugged and let her take it. Frances leaned it against the wall of the gunwale and skipped back into his arms. The musicians laughed and played on while Hermano, and Frances began a staggering kind of waltz.

Joe shook his head in astonishment and all but ran to catch up with Felipe, who was sauntering slowly off to find the hatch to the engine room. The first thing he had to do was to get this so-called mechanic down. He caught the sot reaching for the bottle again and took it away.

"You've got work to do." He punctuated his order with a twist of the arm.

"Jesus, man," Felipe exclaimed, "Just show me the way."

Joe escorted him into the shadows and around to the port side. Taking his tiny flashlight from his pocket, he switched it on and led them down to the engine room. Switching on the battery-powered emergency light on the bulkhead, Joe glared at this miserable excuse for an engineer, hoping he was sober enough. Felipe looked around and seemed transformed.

"Oh yeah, a big Catty 3512," Felipe said with unexpected clarity. "And there's a 385 generator. Looks to be in good shape too." He stepped up on the metal catwalk and walked around the engine inspecting. "Now all we need is some juice in the batteries." He knelt down and opened some valves. "Seawater cooling system. Actually seawater cools the Freon coolant." He stood up, grabbing a handhold to steady himself, and weaved over to pull out the oil dipstick. "Got lube," he said. "Could stand a change, but anyway, it'll do. We had a system like this on the *Okaloosa Minnie*. I remember one time off the coast of Haiti…"

"Look," Joe shouted. "We got no time for stories. Shut up and get this thing going, will ya?"

"Sure, man, keep your shirt on. You don't just turn the key like it was a friggin' car." He made his way around, turning more valves and reading gauges. "Look's like we got some juice in the batteries, anyway." Then he went to the control panel and held down the preheat button. "Okay, here goes."

The engine groaned and turned over weakly a few times. Felipe let go the starter button. "Not getting fuel."

Joe let out his breath. "What can we do?"

"Plenty of fuel in the tanks. The line must need bleeding." Felipe moved around the engine, tracing the line from the injectors. "Get me an adjustable wrench," he commanded. Drunk or not, he was all business. Joe spotted a workbench, opened a couple of drawers and grabbed up a wrench.

"How about this?"

"Okay." He took the wrench and went to the line that came in about chest high. He found a coupling and loosened it, separating the line. "Here, I need you to hold this while I try to pump the air out. He showed Joe how to cover the supply side with his hand. "Put pressure on it while I crank the starter."

Nervous about what was happening on deck, Joe put his hand over the pipe as shown. "Hurry up, will ya."

"Look man, I'm doing the best I can. Now hold the fucker." He pushed the starter.

"I can't feel anything," Joe said impatiently.

"Let go a second. Then be ready to hold it again." He pushed the starter again.

Joe released and was about to clamp his hand back down when a huge burst of fuel sprayed out, soaking Joe's shirt and pants. "Shit!" he cried, letting go and backing away.

"That's got it." Felipe said. He came back with the wrench, shoved Joe out of the way, and refastened the coupling.

Joe began to feel a hot, then a burning sensation, first through his shirt and then through his pants. "The damn fuel," he said. "It itches, burns! Oh, crap!"

"Better get those clothes off," Felipe advised. He was back at the control panel. "Here goes." He pushed the starter. The engine turned over slowly as if the batteries were about gone. Then there was a boom and a roar as the engine fired and ran.

"Damn, almighty damn!" Joe shouted over the din of the engine sound. But as he thrilled to the engine running, he realized he was getting burned. "Ahh. Holy shit!" He pulled up his shirt front. Even in the dimness of the battery-powered lights, he could see red splotches on his stomach. One second it burned; the next second it itched.

"Generator's going," Felipe exclaimed proudly. "Go switch on the master in the power box. We'll see if this fucker's got lights." He turned around to see Joe's fuel-soaked clothes, gave a look of surprise and then grinned. "Got a bath, did ya?"

"Go to hell," Joe told him. He found the power box nearby, opened it and decided to turn off most switches before throwing the main. Once done, he flipped the big breaker and began turning on each individual one. Lights could be coming on all over the ship, he supposed, but couldn't know for sure being below decks. The engine room suddenly illuminated.

"Ship's power grid is okay. All right, man, I got you going. Now what're we gonna do?"

Joe grabbed at his sodden pants, checking to be sure his wallet and phone were there. "You just be ready to answer all bells, you hear?" he commanded.

"Hey, look man, I didn't say I was going with you. I only agreed to get this baby started up. I'm going ashore."

Joe held up the wrench and shook it at him. "You try to leave this engine room and I'll crack your skull and make bloody jello of your stupid brains," he threatened, shaking the wrench at Felipe's head. "You hear me? Just keep the engine going and give me all you got when I order it." His skin was beginning to tingle and burn.

Felipe opened his mouth to protest. Joe raised the big wrench as if to strike. The now very sober engineer shrank back a step. "Okay. Whatever you say. Jesus, man. Okay."

"You just tend the engine. If I see you topside, I'll kill you." Joe was very uncomfortable now. He turned and went up the ladder, having no idea what he would do next.

• CHAPTER SEVENTEEN •

When he reached the door to the main deck, Joe opened it and stepped out. A gust of wind blew across the deck, accompanied by a metallic screeching sound as the aluminum gangway scraped on the concrete dock. He realized there was no longer any music being played. The musicians were rushing down the gangway. The old guard had his hands in the air. Mary and Marsha stood behind Frances, who was aiming the AK 47 rifle at Hermano. A rumbling sound of the idling engine came from the stack. Painfully irritated by the fuel, he considered raiding the crew's quarters for some clothes, but obviously there was no time. Deciding he'd just have to stand it, he hurried over to them.

"Joe! Your clothes are wet? What?

"Damn diesel fuel all over me."

"Oh no, I'm so sorry!" Mary exclaimed and handed him the pistol. "Do I hear the engine running?"

"Yes, thank God," he said. Unconsciously, he was doing a little two-step to combat the burn.

Frances looked at him curiously. "Do you have to go to the bathroom?"

"Never mind," Joe said, standing on one foot and then the other. He exchanged glances with Hermano, who still had his hands up. "How did y'all…?"

"A little distraction," Frances boasted. "Works every time."

"Those musicians ran when Frances got the gun," Mary said.

"They might call the police," Marsha warned. She noticed Joe's strange movements. "What are you doing?"

Joe was twisting like Chubby Checker but couldn't stand it any longer. He pulled the shirt over his head and dropped it on the deck.

"¿*Qué diablo*?" Hermano said, letting his hands down. "Why did you start the engine?" He paused as the sound of a distant siren grew even closer.

There was the sound of a truck driving up, sounding just like Hosea's old jalopy. Joe went to peer over the side. *God, he was burning!* Down on the dock, Hosea got out of the truck, and eight other people were climbing out of the back.

"*Hola*, Joe. You have taken the ship, *si*?" Hosea yelled. He waited a moment for an answer. Then he started for the gangway and motioned vigorously for the people to follow. As they began climbing the gangway stairs, the ship inched away from the dock in a gust of wind and made a screeching sound as the foot of the gangway scraped on the concrete pier.

Joe started to protest but he could only think about the burning. Nothing mattered now but to get the fuel-soaked clothes off.

"It's killing me!" He laid the pistol down, kicked off his shoes, unzipped and stepped out of his pants.

"Joe? What? What are you doing? Mary said. But Joe was incensed. The underpants were sodden with diesel fuel as well. He jerked them off with a little double hop. Marsha let out a little scream.

"*Loco*," Hermano said. "*Hombre loco!*"

Amid exclamations from the ladies, Joe could not help but turn away and rub his reddened parts for a second. "I'm sorry," he murmured and picked up his Glock. Another gust of wind blew, offering a little comfort to his bare skin.

"Look," Frances said, having forgotten to keep the rifle pointed at

Hermano. "Now Joe's got two pistols, see. I always wondered about you. Just look, Mary, he's an exhibitionist if ever…"

"Diesel fuel's burning, itching so bad." he blurted at her. Still in some pain, he looked for something to cover himself. There was nothing. He had no time for modesty.

"Mary, are all the lines off?"

"Yes. But the gangway is…" She was interrupted by the shrieks of the two women who had reached the top of the gangway with their men and had seen Joe. Hosea looked at Joe in surprise and spoke up.

"We're going with you, Señor Joe. But why are you naked?"

"You can't go with us," Joe shouted at him, self-consciously holding the pistol over his parts. Frances handed the rifle to Marsha. The wail of sirens was getting much closer.

"Here," Frances said. She pulled up her skirt and began pulling off her ruffled bloomer-type pants that were part of her costume, careful to let the skirt down as she went. She stepped out of them very primly and handed them to Joe. "Put these on, you silly, sexy devil, before somebody decides to take advantage."

Joe gladly grabbed the pants, glanced at the frills and pulled them on anyway, finding them a bit small and covering only a bikini-part of his body. Feeling a bit more protected, though the burning was far from over, he began to gather his wits. There was yet another scrape of the bottom of the gangway against the concrete.

"Hosea, I cannot take these people," he shouted and waved the pistol at the smuggler. "Get off the ship now!"

"We must go with you, *señor*," Hosea replied. "This is my wife and my children. And Fernando's family as well. We are in danger if they stay here. You owe me a favor remember? We are going with you."

"*Por favor, Señor Joe*," Hosea's wife spoke up. "It means our future, our lives to us."

Joe glanced at Mary to see what she thought and was answered by a very positive nod.

"They must really mean it," Marsha said.

"Anybody who wants to go to sea with some idiot in ruffled panties ought to get to, I imagine," Frances declared.

Joe shrugged. "Okay, Hosea, you win," he replied, "But I can't guarantee anything." He was interrupted by another screech of the gangway as a gust shoved the ship outward a bit. He looked at Hermano.

"I guess you know by now that we're taking this ship to the United States. It's time now for you to just go quietly." He motioned at the gangway. Hermano peered over the side and looked at Joe for a long moment.

"And what do you think they will do to me for letting you go?" he asked. "My duty was to guard the ship, and I have failed."

"Prison time is the most he can hope for," Hosea said. He went over to Hermano. "My profession is taking people across to Florida, *amigo*. My organization in Miami can help you, just as it will help my family find a new life." He was interrupted by the screech of tires and the sirens as two police cars raced out onto the pier and slammed on their brakes. Policemen began piling out, with Maria among them, pointing at the ship.

"To the bridge, quick!" Joe yelled and took off across the deck. He reached the stairs on the port side and climbed three steps at a time. Throwing open the door to the pilot house, he ran to the helm. Beside it was the engine order telegraph. Joe shoved it to "all ahead full", thought a second, and ordered 1/3 ahead. Deciding not to turn on any lights, he shouted the order in the intercom to Felipe when he heard the engine revving up.

"Look alive, mano," he yelled into the intercom. "I'm counting on you."

Mary, Marsha and Frances burst in the door behind him.

"The police are about to come up the gangway," Mary said. "They have guns drawn."

Joe turned the wheel to the right, thinking to shove the bow into the dock and swing the stern out. He sensed the ship begin to move and heard the screeching sound of the gangway. He turned to the ladies.

"Have you got Hermano's rifle?" Frances held it up. Joe nodded, at least they had that and the pistol. He went over to the bridge window on the starboard side and peered down at the dock. Two or three uniformed figures were climbing cautiously up the gangway. Then the bow hit the pier with a heavy thud. Joe ran back and ordered "back 2/3rds" on the engine.

"Mary, watch to see if any of them get aboard," he shouted. Mary ran over to look.

"A policeman's almost at the top," she wailed. The screeching was louder. Then there was a loud heavy bang that shook the ship.

"He fell!" Mary shouted. "I think the gangway collapsed and he fell!"

Joe flung the telegraph arm to all back full and spun the wheel back to amidships. The bow scraped the pier for a second and was soon clear. The ship backed away. There was splashing and yelling in the water beside the pier. Then a couple of shots. The glass in the starboard window shattered. Mary screamed and bolted away from it.

"Everybody stay down," Joe said. He peered out and judged he had enough maneuvering room. Ordering full speed ahead, he spun the wheel to the left and, as the heading swung left, he steadied up and aligned with channel buoys.

"We need the harbor chart," he said. "Mary, come take the wheel. Steer on that light up ahead."

"I don't know how to steer a ship," she protested.

"It's just like steering Alex's sailboat," he said. "You can do it."

"I sure can if she can't," Frances said. "Alex had me chained to that helm for God knows how many endless hours of sailing. I wish he were here now, though. He'd just love all this intrigue and shooting and all. Why I recall that time two years ago in the Bahamas..."

"Quiet, Frances, please," Joe said. "We've got other things to think about."

"Okay, fancy pants," she replied. "I do wish I had my camera now. You're such a dainty, pretty sight."

Joe looked down at his bare and still-burning chest and stomach for just a moment and then forgot the pain again.

"Marsha," he said. "I need you to keep a lookout for any ships or boats or anything."

"Well, I have done that before," she said. "That was the one thing my ex let me do on that sorry banana boat."

"Good girl," Joe said. "I'll be back in just a second." He went out the door of the bridge and climbed cautiously down the steps, pistol in hand. At the bottom, he looked around the corner at the deck. On a hatch cover sat Hermano, Hosea and his eight charges.

"Did any policemen or soldiers or whatever get aboard?" he called.

"No, Joe," Hosea answered. "You very neatly dropped them all in the drink." He laughed.

"Tell us what to do," Hermano said. "We are with you now."

Joe shook his head. "Pray," he said. "Just pray.

CHAPTER EIGHTEEN

Having drifted a hundred yards away from the pier, beyond the accurate aim of the police pistols, and with the ship making way, Joe took a deep breath and began to think of all he had to consider. Should he turn on running lights? Without them, the ship would be harder to see against all the lights of the city, making it something of a black ghost moving through the water. On the other hand, a ship without lights would look more suspicious to anyone who spotted it. Between them and the pass to the sea lay the naval base. Would anyone there be observing passing ships? Lightning struck nearby, illuminating the bridge, followed by booming thunder.

"We'll be seen, lights or no running lights," he mumbled. He scanned the available equipment. There also was an older model surface-search radar, which might be helpful. But it would produce an electronic emission as noticeable as bright lights to a naval vessel's electronic detection equipment. Of course, any ship's radar would detect *Sea Urchin* as a large blip. He found a power switch and set the radar on standby. A timer appeared on the screen showing it would have to count down eight minutes for it to be ready to radiate.

"Joe," Mary said, a nervous quaver in her voice, "Don't you think the police have called their navy or something?" He nodded and glanced back toward the pier.

"The big question is how fast can they contact any coast guard. They may not be that coordinated in their communications. With this being the biggest holiday of the year, maybe the rum is flowing as fast on the naval base as it was on the streets." He scanned the naval docks with his binoculars. Another lightning flash lit up the piers. In its illumination he saw no sign of any ship preparing to get underway and give chase.

"The one thing we have on our side is the element of surprise," he said. "Time is on our side."

"Thank goodness for that," Frances said. "But we better hurry up."

"Marsha," Joe said, trying to keep a cool demeanor—the discipline he had learned as s naval officer. "See that electrical panel behind you. Find the switch marked 'running lights'." She hurried over and searched through the box, found the switch and flipped it.

"Running lights should be on," she announced. A heavy wind gust whistled through the shot-out window.

"That storm's still coming," Joe said. Raising the binoculars to his eyes, he took another look ahead, then glanced at the compass.

"Mary, come right to three-one-zero." He watched her turn the wheel. "Not quite so much rudder," he advised. "Small course changes take small amounts of rudder. Less wheel-turning." He watched the compass. "Okay, now steady up." He saw she was getting the hang of it. She surely had been great on the helm of Alex's sixty-foot boat that time they sailed in the storm in the Abacoe.

At night it was difficult to sight navigation buoys because behind them were the bright lights of Viejo Havana across the bay. Occasional lightning flashes were little help. He was glad he had studied the chart the night before when he had slipped aboard, and he hoped his memory was good. He anticipated a right turn in a few hundred yards to the channel course heading toward the sea.

"Frances, see if you can help Marsha find the running light switches," he said. The portside door to the bridge opened and Hosea stepped inside.

"*Hasta ahora todo bien, si* Joe?" he said.

"So far so good." He made a cursory introduction to Mary and Frances. "Hosea is responsible for finding us our drunken engineer,"

"I just checked on him," Hosea said. "You have never seen a happier mano—throttle in one hand, Havana Club in the other." He laughed. "Somehow he found a moment to raid the crates in the hold."

"So Hosea, tell me about these people you've brought on board," Joe demanded while keeping his attention on the course ahead.

"It's my wife and our son, his wife and children, and Fernando's wife and daughter."

"Well, who the hell gave you the right to bring them aboard?"

"With Fernando in jail, we all are in danger of being arrested as well," he explained. "This was the favor I had asked of you," Hosea replied. He caught another glimpse of Joe still wearing nothing but Frances' frilly underpants and chuckled. "Remember, I provided you with the engineer. And clearly our *muchacho* Felipe is doing his job, no? *Inebriato* or not."

"I hope they know what danger you've put them in?" Joe replied. "Who knows how all of this will turn out." He walked over and checked the timer on the radar. It showed another four minutes until ready to work. "Mary, have you seen the flashing lights on the buoys?"

"There are so many lights up there in the city," she said, standing on her tip toes as if to help her see better. Joe picked out the momentary flash of a green light, counted by thousands until it flashed again.

"See if you can spot that green light just above the water. It's flashing every four seconds." He pointed. "Then on our starboard side we should see a red flashing light on a buoy."

"I haven't seen it yet," Mary admitted, craning her neck to view.

Joe strained to see through the binoculars. He caught a glimpse of the red one coming into view on their right side. "Just steer a little more to the right. Let's try three-one-five. Wait until I tell you to turn." He glanced at Frances. "Have you seen any shipping? Keep a good eye. Let me know if anything is moving."

"Aye, aye, Cap'n Fancypants," Frances said. "And what happens if we do spot something? Those policemen back at the pier are not too happy, let me tell you, especially those that got an unexpected swim. I guess you'll tell them it was just an accident." Ignoring Frances, he turned back to Hosea.

"Where are all your people now?" Joe asked.

"They are in the crew's mess," Hosea said, "along with our new friend, Hermano."

"I hope he's our friend," Joe replied. "Keep an eye on him, will you? He is a good man, but he also is a soldier."

"*Si, capitán*," Hosea said. He made a saluting gesture, which Joe took as sincere, and went out on deck. The Cuban started down the ladder but was accosted by Hermano, who had come up to the outer bridge. Joe noted the two talking earnestly and worried about what the old guard was thinking. Perhaps he was having second thoughts.

"Frances, where is Hermano's rifle?" Joe asked.

"It's over there," she said, gesturing toward the corner behind the chart table.

"Hide it, will you. Probably nothing to worry about, but I don't want the old man to find it." She nodded and went over to take care of it. A really bright lightning flash lit up the bay.

"I think we're coming close to a buoy or something," Marsha said. She was looking out to starboard. Realizing he had been distracted, Joe rushed over to look and arrived at her side just as another lightning flash lit up a very close green-lighted buoy. Then he lost sight of it as it became obscured under the port bow, too close for comfort. He was about to shout to Mary to turn left but realized it would only swing the stern more to the right. Then there was a loud scraping sound along the hull on the starboard side.

"Shit," Joe said. "We've hit their fucking buoy." He looked up to see another green-lighted buoy a hundred yards ahead. The awful scraping sound from the struck buoy moved on toward the aft part of the ship.

"Right full rudder," he commanded, looking at Mary. She gave him a blank look.

"What?"

"Turn the wheel to the right," he shouted. "Turn it, turn it." Mary gave the helm a good spin until it reached its stops. Joe looked out to see the heading slowly begin to change to the right. "Okay, turn the wheel back to the left. Just about halfway. Okay, we're turning. The channel course is three-five-zero. Steady on that course." Then he noted that the ship was turning too quickly. "Put the rudder amidships, quick." He could see Mary was confused. He ran over and took the wheel from her, turning it back to the left to stop the turn. Then he steadied up on the channel heading.

"Okay, Mary dear," he said, wiping perspiration off his forehead. "Take it back now and steer three-five-zero by the compass." She looked at him, shook her head, sighed and gingerly took the wheel again.

"You're doing fine," he said. "Don't worry, you can handle it." He pointed to the next red-lighted marker. "Just steer so as to keep that light just off your starboard bow, okay." He gave her a little pat on the shoulder. "it'll be all right."

"All right, huh?" Frances said as she peered out of the porthole into the darkness. "That sure looks like the running lights of a ship up ahead, coming straight for us."

Joe jerked the binoculars up to his eyes to see. It was a ship all right, a cutter by the look of it, standing in the channel toward them at a good speed. It did not look like a merchantman. A bright lightning flash briefly illuminated the vessel. No, it was some kind of naval ship; he could see a gun mount on its bow.

Hermano opened the pilot house door. "*¿Puedo entrar?*"

"*Hermano, si, amigo, ven a buscar,*" Joe said. "*¿Es un barco de la marina?*"

"*Si,*" Hermano said gravely. "It's a coastal patrol ship."

"Do they have guns?" Marsha asked. "Like cannons or something." Her voice was nearly in falsetto.

"Probably," Joe admitted. Staring through the binoculars, he watched the two ships closing on one another. He could see that the turreted gun on the cutter's deck was at least a three-incher. It could blow the bridge off his ship with one shot and take all of them with it. He had a flashback to his time as Tactical Action Officer on the guided missile frigate. *Weaps, Mount Fifty-one battery released. Destroy Target Alpha.*

Then, back to the present, he realized ruefully, tonight the other ship was the cat, and he was only the mouse.

"Suppose they try to stop us," Marsha said. "Can they stop us?"

"They can fire their big gun," Hermano said. "We are quite helpless, no?"

"What do I do?" Mary wailed. "Do I just keep steering toward them?"

Joe took another quick look at the approaching vessel. There was no indication of the cutter being ready for any action. He gritted his teeth. *There's only one way.* He ran to the engine order telegraph and shoved the levers forward.

"Full speed ahead," he shouted in the voice tube to the engine room, thinking he would ring the neck of that sot down there if he didn't get every rpm out of that diesel. Thankfully, there was a cheery reply.

"*Ella ronronea como un gatito y puede rugir como un león,*" Felipe called back. The engine indeed roared like a lion as he advanced the throttle.

"What are you doing, Joe?" Marsha asked.

"All I know how," he said. "Just charging straight ahead, roaring like a lion, and hoping for the best." There were some gasps followed by silence as the deck began to vibrate in the acceleration.

"Not much of a plan," Frances spoke up. "Is that the best you can do, Captain Fancypants?"

Joe shrugged. "God knows I wish I knew. I'm open to any ideas."

"I just wish we had stayed at the dock," Marsha said. "Everybody was drinking, and we were snockered at least."

"Just celebrating the Revolution," Mary said. Frances suddenly threw up her hands.

I know, I know!" she shouted. "Let's go find some more whiskey bottles and have another party. Goodness knows, if we're going to be blown to smithereens and arrested and thrown in some sorry ole Cuban jail, I say let's have a ball doing it."

As she spoke, her resolve grew. "Come on everybody. Let's go back down on deck and have a party. You can handle the ship can't you, Cap'n Fancy? Sure you can. Come on, girls." She grabbed Hermano by the arm. "Come on you sexy old Cuban commie, you. Let's go down and break out the rum." She tugged at Hermano. "What've we got to lose?"

"Frances, really!" Mary said. "How can we..."

"Oh, what the hell, Mary?" Frances insisted. "Let's get Hosea and his Cubans to come join us. We'll have a big time." Mary gave Frances a quizzical stare, and then her face lightened.

"Maybe if we look like a party boat," Mary said, looking at Joe. "If we look like a group that's having a good time like all those people in Havana, then maybe the coast guard will let us alone."

Joe shook his head. "Why not?" He looked at Hermano. "Can you join in?"

"Sure he can," Frances was taking control. "Come on let's do it. Hurry!" She waved them on out of the pilot house. Hermano and Marsha followed her down to the main deck.

Joe looked at Mary. "Go try to control Frances, dear. I can handle the ship."

"Control Frances? I wish I could. We wouldn't be here now if I were able to do that. But I'll do the best I can. Are you sure you are all right?"

"Of course," Joe said, not really believing he had a handle on anything at the moment. "Just go try to make something sensible out of whatever Frances is up too, okay?"

"I love you, Joe."

"I love you, Mary." Joe gave her a quick embrace. "I'm sorry we're in such a mess." She gave him a big hug and hurried out. Joe watched her go and then turned his attention back to steering the ship. In order to stay in the channel, he would have pass the cutter very close aboard to port. All he could hope for was that the word of their taking the ship had not yet reached the incoming ship. Maybe the holiday spirit of Revolution Day was keeping their guard down. He glanced down at the port side deck and saw Frances waving her arms, calling everyone to join her.

"Lord help us," he muttered. "No telling what she's up to."

• • •

As Mary made it down the stairs to the main deck, she could hear Frances barking orders.

"Listen everyone. We're having a party, *comprende*? Hosea, tell your family we're celebrating Revolution Day, *savvy*?"

The family members, who apparently spoke no English, wore

expressions of common bewilderment and not a little fear. Mary could see that they were somewhat intrigued by Frances, however, this gringo woman in a flashy ruffled dress, yelling out orders to everyone including the men. Hosea translated for them, but since Frances shouted in English, likely it seemed much more exotic.

"Marsha, go find those bottles we had," Frances went on. "Didn't Joe say this ship was loaded with rum? And who knows a song? Surely the revolution had some songs about Castro and all the commies and whatever else they all celebrate." She waved her hands as if conducting.

"*Allons enfants de tree vion…* Oh wait, that's French. Come on, Hosea, get something started for us. A good ole gut-busting Cuban something."

Hosea was looking at how close the cutter was to them. He shrugged and began a tentative few words of the anthem.

Al combate corred bayameses que la patria os contempla orgullosa
No temais una muerte gloriosa…

"Everybody now," Frances said, waving and coaxing the Cubans to sing. "Ooh, not so much about the "glorious death" part. Look, how about that *Guantanamera* song. Oh good, here comes Marsha. Pass those bottles around, dear. We've got to get tipsy again. Marsha, don't you know some good songs? Goodness knows you've lived here long enough."

"Knowing songs and being able to sing are two different things," Marsha replied. "Look, you don't even want to hear."

As Frances argued briefly with Marsha, Mary glanced nervously at the approaching ship, now not much more than a hundred yards away. Obviously, it would pass close. Then from the cutter came a very bright light. The Cuban navy crew had switched on a searchlight and were training it on them. Everybody froze and stared at the light.

"Okay," Frances yelled. "Showtime! Let's go, everybody.

Guantanamera. Guajia Guantanamera..." She waved her arms. Let's go. Sing, dance, carouse, party, party, party." She grabbed Hermano by the arm. "Hermano, come dance with me, you sexy old goat! Show me how to rhumba. Come on, Mary, grab a partner. And sing, everybody, sing!"

Somehow the group came alive. They got into the act, and show-time it was. As the two ships passed one another at a range of fifty yards, Frances waved a rum bottle at their bridge. Once out of the cutter's spotlight, Mary could see the silhouettes of men standing at the rail, all armed with rifles, but some were waving, and she thought she heard laughter. It all took only a minute and then the stern of the cutter went on past and the distance between the ships opened. But the refugees sang on, with more vigor, as if they had defied the enemy and escaped. When the song finished, Frances led them all in a self-congratulatory applause.

"All right, you people." Frances said. "Good work. We showed 'em, didn't we? Say, Hermano, you're not a bad dancer after all." She pulled him close and gave him a kiss on the cheek.

"*¿Traes pila?*" he ventured gamely. "*¿Un mate?*"

"Watch it, buster!" Frances exclaimed. "I am a married woman."

Mary was still watching the other ship, illuminated by a lightning flash. Sensing some relief, she realized perhaps they had not seen the last of the cutter. Huge raindrops suddenly began pelting her.

With squeals and yelps, Hosea and family, Frances and Marsha, and Hermano rushed to the cover of the crew's quarters. Mary ran up the stairs to the pilot house to assist Joe with whatever might happen next.

• CHAPTER NINETEEN •

The storm arrived. Wind driven huge raindrops pelted the ship. Torrents of water cascaded down the bridge windows obscuring view. He could just make out Mary running to the bridge. Rain gushed in from the shot-out window on the starboard side of the bridge. Mary had opened the door when the wind hit, slamming her against the bulkhead and then to the deck of the pilot house. Abandoning the helm for a moment, Joe rushed to help her up.

"Are you okay?" he asked as he returned to the wheel. She nodded and regained her footing. Joe ran back to the wheel, which was spinning off-course. He tried to see the channel buoys ahead, but they now were obscured by sheets of rain. Looking at the radar repeater, he made out the two lines of buoys and steered back into the channel course and hoped he was at the center of it.

"Come take the helm," he shouted over the deafening sound of wind coming in the broken window. Mary made her way over beside him.

"Just steer the course by the compass," he ordered. "I'll watch the radar."

"I'll try," she said as she rubbed her arm, apparently hurting where the wildly swinging door had hit her. Marsha and Frances came up the interior stairway to the pilot house.

"Where's the Cuban ship?" Frances asked. "It's not coming after us, I hope."

"Can't say yet," Joe replied. He went to the radar unit, which was near enough to the window to be wet. Thankfully, it was housed in a waterproof console. The greenish-yellow beam which rotated around in the screen showed little but a lot of rain and sea return. Nervously, he tried adjusting the gain and brightness, turning them up too much so that the screen was all snow. With trembling fingers, he forced himself to make smaller corrections with the knobs and tuning more carefully. Although there was a lot of clutter from the radiation bouncing off ever higher sea waves, he managed to make out the blips of the nearest buoys ahead. He switched on the ship's-head marker and saw a green line shoot out from the center of the scope. It intersected the line of blips on the right.

"Mary, turn left," he ordered. "Not much. Try twenty degrees."

"You mean turn the wheel left twenty degrees or steer a course twenty degrees to the left?"

"Turn the wheel about halfway around," he said, struggling to remain calm. "Now hold that 'til I tell you." He watched the cursor on the scope a few moments. "Okay, now rudder amidships. Bring it back to the top. You got it. What's your compass heading?" He was trying not to sound exasperated.

"Looks like about three-two-zero. Will that do?"

"Fine. Just hold that for a few minutes."

"Have you looked back at that ship we passed? Are they going to turn around and chase us?" Marsha asked. Her voice broke a little when she asked.

"We'll see," Joe replied. He increased the range on the radar screen so he could see the ship and set the range cursor on it. It would take a few minutes to determine what that ship was doing. He studied the relative movement of the line of buoys. "We can turn back right to our original course of three-two-five. Just make a slow turn correction since you don't want to change direction very much." The ship began to pitch as it passed Morro Castle and entered the sea.

"I wish you would take this wheel," Mary said. "I don't..."

"Listen, you're doing great. Remember what a great job you did during the hurricane coming back from the Bahamas."

"Boy, do I remember," Frances said. "I sure hope this storm's not anything like that one."

"This one's just a squall, I think," Joe assured her. "Should be over soon." He did watch intensely, however, to be certain Mary was able to hold the course, which apparently she was. He walked over to the port window and peered out. After the performance they put on for the Cuban navy, Hosea and family had run for shelter—to the salon two levels down, he guessed. *What was he going to do with them?* he wondered. That is if he did manage to take the ship out to the twelve-mile limit.

He went back to check the radar. The heading marker was now pointing nicely between the lines of buoys, showing they were safely in the channel and soon would pass the sea buoy.

"As best I can tell from this rain-cluttered radar picture," he said. "The Cuban ship seems to be entering the naval base. Oh man, are we lucky!"

"Does that mean we're safe?" Marsha asked.

"No other fools but us would be out at sea in this," Frances assured her.

"The rain's letting up some," Mary said. I think we're about to pass another set of buoys."

"Checks out with the radar," Joe replied and confirmed with a look through the binoculars. "You seem to be right on course."

They heard footfalls on the steps. Hosea and Hermano entered the bridge, dripping wet.

"*Qué pasa,* Joe?" Hosea asked.

"Eleven miles to go, amigo," he said. "Can't tell you any more than that. I don't think those navy boys are going to give us any trouble, but we're not clear yet."

"You saw how fast they entered port," Hosea said. "It looked as if they were late for Revolution Day festivities."

"I doubt they'll bother us," Hermano said. "If the government cared much for this ship, they would have had better guards than I." No one replied. The silence told their thoughts. The old soldier shook his head.

"I have been played for the fool," he said. "My honor is ruined." Marsha went over and put her hand on his arm.

"Don't be so hard on yourself," she said.

"I'm sorry you feel that way, Hermano," Joe said. "But if these ladies had not tricked you, amigo, I don't know what we'd have done."

"After my wife died, I have had no real life," Hermano said with a shrug. "Perhaps it is Providence that brought me to this."

"*La providencia puede ser buena fortuna,*" Hosea told him.

"Good fortune. I hope you're right, Hosea," Joe said. "Say, would you go down to the engine room and check on old Felipe. So far, he's kept things running great, but that in itself worries me."

"*Entiendo,*" Hosea nodded. "You okay up here?"

"With this helmsman, how could I go wrong?" He smiled at Mary. She glanced at him and did not smile back. Her sudden change in demeanor surprised him.

"Don't patronize me, Joe Anderson," she said after Hosea had left. "I'll have a few things to say to you if we ever get out of this."

Joe grimaced. "I'm so sorry that you're having to go through all of this," he said. *But it wasn't my idea that you came to Cuba.* He wanted to add but knew better. Her change of tone from frightened to peeved was a good thing, in a way. Silently, he went back to look at the radar. "Steer just a couple of degrees more to the left, Mary dear," he said.

Now that the storm had brought with it much cooler air, Joe

began to shiver and then realized he still had on nothing more than Frances' frilly pants.

"I wonder if anybody can find me some clothes."

"You just don't worry about that until we get twelve miles out," Frances fussed. "Look at us. We've got a drunken sot down there running the engines and a naked exhibitionist up here acting like a captain. It'll be a wonder if we can survive all of this. Where are we anyway?"

"That's the sea buoy up ahead," Joe said, indicating the outermost channel marker. "If we keep up this speed and our luck holds, we'll be twelve miles out in about thirty more minutes."

"Well, I have a good feeling about it now," Frances replied. "But I'm still praying."

Joe ran the scan range out on the radar again to check for contacts. "It's hard to believe, but nobody is pursuing us." All at once he realized he was terribly cold and began trembling. It was now after midnight. He had been wound so tight emotionally, relief nearly made him collapse. He went over to Mary and gave her a hug from behind.

"Well, I see you two obviously need a break," Frances said. "Here, let me drive this thing." She went over and stood behind Mary, watching her steer by the compass.

"Oh, would you please take over," Mary asked. "I've been staring at that compass so long, I'm getting cross-eyed."

"Sure, honey. Let me have it." Frances stepped up to the wheel and took over. "Alex always makes me steer his old *Mission* while he goes for a ten-minute nap. Then he stays in bed for an hour or two." She stared at the compass and turned the wheel expertly. "Yes, I've got the hang of this baby. Hosea, honey, you'll stay and help, won't you?"

"Let me take it for a while if you please," Hosea said. "Then I will need to go down below with my wife." He stepped up to the wheel and took it from Frances. She jumped up in the captain's chair.

"Go on, you two," she waved Joe and Mary away. "Go find Joe some decent clothes, you ole devil. I've seen a way lot more than I want of Cap'n Fancypants."

"If you have any problems," Joe said with a grin, "just pull on that cord above you to sound the whistle, and I'll come running."

"Go on," Frances replied. "You're the only problem I know of around here, going off on this crazy CIA mission to Cuba and making Mary and me have to come find you and save your rear end. Looks like you'd learn. Ah well, I never could teach Alex anything either. He's always off doing some stock fraud deal or something. Men, men, men."

"Thank you, Frances," Joe said.

Mary led the way down to the captain's cabin. He held the door for her and tried to give her a quick kiss as she entered. She resisted. He turned to lock the door when she let him have it.

"Just who do you think you are, Joe Anderson? Going off on this escapade after promising me, PROMISING ME that you'd never go on another. Do you realize just how close we've all come to being shot by the police or being arrested and put in jail?" Her tirade was causing him to back up.

She kept coming toward him, angrily in his face. He backed into the side of the bed, and she gave him a hardy push. Joe fell back, and Mary suddenly laughed with glee, threw up the hem of her Cuban costume and fell upon him.

"And get those frilly pants off, you silly devil." She grabbed and pulled them down. He laughed and reached for her panties. They held one another and kissed longingly. Mary rolled over on him and they made love as if they were starving for one another—youthful, wild, passionate love. And then curled up together in the narrow bunk, they slept.

• • •

AT DAWN AS BRIGHT SUNLIGHT shone through the porthole, they awoke, happy and rested.

"I love you so much," Joe said in breathless ecstasy. He held her to him tightly and found her lips with his. They lay still in their embrace, absorbing the being of one another.

"While I was feeling so lost in Cuba," Joe said softly. "I was beginning to think I would never hold you again. I cannot imagine why I went off on this crazy fool mission." He hugged her tightly and kissed her neck.

"You're an idiot, a maniac, a fool, and a downright adorable nut," she said. "Just too much testosterone, I guess." She playfully reached down and squeezed where such fluids reputedly are generated.

"Ow!" he said and gave her a nip on the nipple.

"Ouch yourself," she cried. They caressed and kissed, and then they heard a loud toot on the ship's whistle.

"Oh, no," Mary exclaimed. "What was that?"

"Frances is calling us. Gosh, no wonder. She's been on the helm for hours." Joe swung his legs over the bed and stood up. "Help me find some clothes, quick."

They frantically opened drawers and the closet. Mary found some underwear and t-shirt and tossed them to him. Then from the captain's remote speaker the VHF radio hissed.

"*Sea Urchin, Sea Urchin,* this is United States Coast Guard Cutter *Intrepid,* over."

Then Frances' unmistakable voice replied. "This is *Sea Urchin. Over.*"

"We are here to escort you to Miami. Over."

"Now look here, Coast Guard, we are a spy ship with all kinds of secret stuff on board, and we just came from Havana. That's in Cuba, you know. And speaking of Cuba, have we got some really great rum aboard this little ole ship; I can tell you for a fact from my personal experience. So we're doing just dandy. over."

"Request to speak to your captain, over."

"Well, he's not available. He and his lovely, nice lady are down in the captain's cabin at present. Now I certainly do not approve of such things, but they are planning to be married, so I guess it's all right. I mean I wasn't brought up that way, but things do change, and I won't object. And you certainly need not mind. See she's repossessing him, so to speak, just as he has repossessed this ship for the CIA, but I'm not supposed to talk about that. We can find our own way to Miami, so you all just go on about your business. Maybe you can catch some old drug runners or something, and not bother us. And don't get too close because I don't steer this big thing so well. So roger dodger, wilco and see ya' later alligator."

There was a click, a silence, and then, "Intrepid, roger, out."

Joe couldn't believe it. "Do you suppose she got away with that?"

"She always does," Mary laughed. "Come on, let's go relieve her so she can rest."

"I'll be right behind you," Joe replied. Mary nodded and headed for the bridge.

Joe discovered a pair of khaki pants that were close enough to his size and got them on. Not bothering to find shoes, he charged on toward the bridge, buttoning and zipping on the way. When he arrived in the pilot house, he saw the cutter steaming away to the west. Mary and Hosea were there, and Hosea had taken the wheel to relieve Frances.

"Okay, it's my turn to take a rest," Frances said. "You'd better do some navigating, Joe, since I ran the Coast Guard away."

"Well, I'm glad you felt so confident in our ability to sail on to port," he laughed.

"Listen, Captain Fancy—I guess we can't call you that anymore since you've put on some decent clothes—anyway, as I was saying, if we can get out of Havana, we can sure get to Miami. Of course, you'd never have made it if Mary and I hadn't been there to help you. So don't think you're so great, Fancypants."

"As angry as I was when I saw you two get out of that bicycle taxi, and tipsy at that, I'll have to admit, your guiling performance with Hermano was nothing less than amazing."

"Where is that cute old soldier, anyway?" Frances asked. "And where is that Marsha woman? They were up here earlier and said they were going to find some breakfast."

"Breakfast! What a wonderful idea!" Mary said.

"My wife, Adoncia, and Benita and the others found canned beans, and they are all in the galley making frijoles. They even found some powdered eggs."

"Capitán Joe," Hosea spoke up. "If I may use your phone, I would like to call my contact in Florida. I need to have my Cuban network arrange to have our immigration approved before we arrive."

"I don't know how you do that," Joe said as he handed him his phone, "but be sure you include Hermano and Felipe in whatever you work out."

"*Despacio, amigo.* Fernando and I have connected with many powerful people over the years."

"What about Fernando?" Joe asked. "Will he go to prison?"

"I doubt it," Hosea replied. "CIA will pay the right people to have him and his boy, Chacko, freed."

"I knew you two had some connection with the Agency," Joe said. "I realized that when Fernando was ferrying me to Cuba."

"Unfortunately, his boat has been impounded by the government."

"Oh, don't worry," Frances piped in, "Joe will likely volunteer to go get it. He seems to have a penchant for that sort of thing." It brought a laugh from all.

"Not gonna happen," Joe said smiling. "By the way, Hosea, did you hear what's happened to that sorry rat, Heinz?"

"Si, he is probably on his way to Germany by now."

"Good thing. If he were to show up in the U.S. I might have to strangle the son of a bitch," he said and then thought about his replacement engineer.

"Ahoy, engine room!" he called into the intercom. "You awake down there, Felipe?"

"*Feliz como un mono y un plátano,*" was the reply. "*Me encanta este motor!*"

"What was that?" Mary asked.

"Says, he's happy as a monkey in a banana tree," Joe translated. "And loves the engine," he laughed.

"When I went to check on him," Hosea laughed, Felipe was running about oiling and wiping down all the machines and drunk as a skunk," Hosea laughed. "He's so *loco* over having an engineering plant to care for, he won't even know he's in Miami." Joe supposed that with the cash he had promised Felipe along with the man's engineering experience, he would find another ship to sign on—if he could stay sober long enough.

"So, Hosea," Mary asked, "how will you and your family get along in the United States?"

"There are a number of organizations in Miami to help immigrating Cubans, señora. All of us, even Hermano in his Cuban Revolutionary Army uniform, will be assisted." Hosea looked sad. "What we lost was Fernando's boat. I expect it will remain property of the government." He shook his head. "As smugglers, we were doing important work for the people."

Joe checked the GPS. They were south of the Keys and rounding the tip of Florida. He consulted the chart and reset the GPS to 25° 45' N, 80° 06' W, a point near the Miami sea buoy. He gave Hosea a northerly course to steer.

"We should reach the Gulf Stream soon," the Cuban replied as he changed course to the left.

Mary had been thinking about Hosea's last remark about his human trafficking being important work. He regarded him standing at the helm, steering so deftly, and decided Hosea must have been a seaman most of his life.

"Hosea, even though we have just been through this frightening narrow escape from Cuba, are you going to keep transporting Cuban immigrants?" she asked.

"*Liberadora, señora, por favor.* Hosea replied. "Freeing my people." He paused, thinking. "Let me recite the words from our song, Mary. In the final verse, of Marti's *Guantanamera,* our *Guajitra,* our Cuban peasant, sings, "*Por los pobres de la tierra, quiero yo mi suerta echar.* With the poor people of this earth, I want to share my fate." He hummed the chorus. "You see, Mary, I am inspired by the great José Marti to do what I can for these people." He held his hands in a palms-up gesture.

They were silent for a few minutes. Joe thought about how Hosea, the man whom he first assumed was only a rogue, was really a fine, dedicated person.

Then he looked at Mary, realizing how much he admired her and wanted to make her happy. Yes, her happiness meant more to him than anything. Then an idea came to him and he acted upon it.

"Hosea," he said. "I have an aging trawler sitting unused in a marina up the coast. I would like to lend it to you and Fernando for a while. I believe you two can put it to much better use."

Mary was shocked. And then she was jubilant. "Joe, do you mean it? Really?" He nodded as she rushed to him and flung her arms around his neck.

"I think you and I have had enough sea-going for a while, sweet Mary," Joe said and kissed her. "The idea of going to Birmingham for the rest of the summer sounds wonderful at this point—maybe for the whole year."

"I hope you will make that *forever*!" Mary cried, happy tears in her eyes.

"Forever," Joe said. "At least the being with you part, I mean." He wasn't committing to life in Birmingham forever, but he did intend to be with her for their lifetime.

Hosea had been watching them with amusement. "I will be more than happy to be your best man, *amigo,* should you need one. And I hope you are serious about the trawler. There are many in Cuba who seek my services."

"You'll find it needs a little more work, my friend. But it should serve you well. We'll sign a one-dollar lease for a year and then see where we are."

"*Muy generoso,* Joe. *Muchas gracias!*"

"*De nada, amigo mio,*" Joe replied with a smile and had another idea. He gave Mary another hug then went over to the chart table, digging into the drawers until he found an American flag.

"Mary," he said. "Frances likely is napping in the captain's cabin. Would you please tiptoe in there and find her frilly under panties I had on, and bring them out to the mast?"

"Whatever for?" she asked.

"Just meet me out there and I'll show you."

• • •

JOE MADE HIS WAY aft of the pilot house to the ship's mast. The deck was getting warm from the bright morning sun, and it felt good to his bare feet. After the storms at Havana, it was great to see a beautiful day at sea with the ship leaving a white wake in the deep dark blue water. A school of dolphins appeared, surfacing, diving, playing in the wake at the bow. Mary, still wearing that colorful frilly dress, climbed up to where Joe stood at the base of the mast.

"Here they are," she said. The warm breeze created by the ship moving at fifteen knots blew her blond curls, and she swept them back from her face. She saw Hermano and Marsha at the bow.

"Look, Joe," she cried. "Hermano has his arm around her!"

"Really?" Joe looked. Sure enough, a relationship had been brewing all night. "He's old enough to be her father."

"That Cuban blood runs mighty hot, they say," Mary quipped.

"Well," Joe said, recalling how lonely, how in need of someone, Marsha had seemed. "I'm glad they've found each other." Joe put his arm around Mary and they watched the unlikely couple for a few moments. Mary held up the panties.

"What do you want with these?"

"Just hang on a minute," Joe said, smiling. Turning to the mast and loosening the halyard from a cleat, he clipped on the American flag and hoisted it on the main halyard. He stepped back and saluted.

"Now give them to me," he said. He took the frilly, lacy panties to a second halyard and raised them to the yardarm. Mary clapped and laughed. Joe put his arm around her, and they stood silently looking at the sea. Frances appeared climbing up to join them. She spotted the strange banner blowing in the wind.

"All hail the Fancypants!" she shouted. Her shout attracted the attention of the pair on the bow. They put their hands up to shield their eyes from the bright sun and stared at the fluttering panties.

"What does that signify, *Señor*?" Hermano called.

"It's a repossession flag," Joe quipped. "It means this ship has successfully been repossessed."

Mary took him by the hand and they kissed. Watching them, Frances called out.

"It also means, despite my better judgement and advice, Mary once again has won this wild and crazy Joe Anderson. He too has been repossessed."

As they stood admiring the school of dolphins chasing alongside, Joe sighed. Man, he loved Mary, but he also loved the sea. Yes, he was happy to be going home with Mary to enjoy her elegant and gracious, tamer life. But as he looked across the dark blue ocean, he knew that the sea was not yet finished with him, nor he with her.

THE END

• ABOUT THE AUTHOR •

A resident of Birmingham, Stephen B. Coleman, Jr. (Steve), a graduate of Indian Springs School, earned a Bachelor of Arts in history from Duke University and a Master of Arts in English from University of Alabama. He is married to the former Dr. Sumter M. Carmichael, a psychiatrist. Steve has been a naval officer, a high school teacher, a businessman, and commercial real estate broker. He has published three other novels: *The Navigator: A Perilous Passage, Evasion at Sea* and *The Navigator II: Irish Revenge; André's Reboot: Striving to Save Humanity* has won Honorable Mention from *Writer's Digest*, a Distinguished Favorite 2021 of NYC Big Book Awards, and a Silver Medal by Independent Publisher Book Awards 2020.

To learn more or to reach out to Steve:

www.andretherobot.com | www.captstevestories.com.

steve@captstevestories.com